The Mystery Beneath Midville Museum

Anne Loader McGee

Vendera Publishing

Visit the author online at: www.annemcgee.com

ISBN: 978-1-936307-40-1

Cover art by Ricky Aschbrenner | vilstar09@gmail.com

Cover & Interior Design by Scribe Freelance
www.scribefreelance.com

Other Books By Anne Loader McGee

Kyle stopped his bicycle to stare puzzled into the woods. A wind appeared to be whipping fiercely at the trees, yet he could hear no sound.

"I also read in those books," Mallory continued, "that the soul of the dead person had to pass through lakes of fire and pits filled with snakes before they could get to the afterlife."

"Mallory!" Kyle shouted. "Something's wrong here."

Mallory spun her bike around and rode back to where Kyle stared mesmerized.

A silent ferocious wind was whipping through the foliage. Everything about it felt wrong. "Let's get out of here," Mallory shouted as the forest turned even darker. She jumped back on her bike and pedaled at breakneck speed from the area.

Kyle followed, his heart racing.

Behind them the woods returned to normal.

AcKNoWLedgMeNtS

I would like to thank my dear friend Jean Henry who critiqued the first part of this story but couldn't stay to give her input on the rest of the manuscript. She was a source of great strength and encouragement to me over the years, and there are no words descriptive enough to express how much I will miss her.

As always I am forever grateful to the members of my two writing groups who consistently guide me to improve my stories: Kate Hovey, Anjali Amit, Michael Thal, Susan Schader, and Rachel Brachman. I especially want to thank Susan and Michael who took the time to read and edit the completed manuscript. Their input was invaluable.

To this list of people I also wish to add my son, Ashley McGee. He allows me to use him as a sounding board throughout the writing of my stories, and then patiently and generously edits each completed project. I couldn't do this without him.

And let's not forget my extremely talented illustrator, Ricky Aschbrenner who has once again created an exciting image to grace the cover of Book Three in the Cedar Creek Mystery Series. He is an artist destined for greatness.

I am also eternally grateful to my publisher, Jaime Vendera of Vendera Publishing, and to my interior layout and designer, Daniel Middleton of Scribe Freelance. Thank you both.

To Jean Henry

When the school bus finally grounded to a halt outside the Midville Museum, Mallory Gilmartin stared out the window frowning. The uneasiness that had begun soon after they left Cedar Creek now swept over her in great waves. She turned to tell her friend Kyle Johnson about it, but glassy-eyed and eager, Kyle's only concern was getting into the museum as fast as he could.

Mallory remembered how shy Kyle had been when she, her mother, and brother first moved to the quaint rural town of Cedar Creek, Virginia, but since then he had become her best friend. And now, although they were on a supposed fun field trip to the nearby town of Midville, Mallory could not shake the feeling that something was not quite right about the two story grey stone building standing in the distance.

"Now, students," she heard Mrs. Abigail Romano their eighth grade teacher command from the front, "I want you to depart the bus in an orderly manner and wait in line on the sidewalk until I give the order to move." The dumpy, pear-shaped woman kept strict military order whenever her students were out on field trips and today was no exception.

"Let's go!" Kyle yelled at Mallory. He jumped to his feet,

grabbed his book bag and squeezed into the crowded aisle.

Having decided to make the best of what was obviously going to be a boring field trip, Mallory stood to follow.

"Don't forget," Mrs. Romano called cheerily once they were all lined up outside, "today's trip to the Egyptian Exhibit will be your history assignment for the week. I expect everyone to take lots of notes."

A collective groan sounded behind her.

"And remember to send Joyce Danner's mother a thank-you note for making today's event possible," Mrs. Romano continued as they set off. "We would not be here were it not for her kind efforts."

Joyce Danner, a short doe-eyed girl near the front of the line, did not react to the mention of her name. She simply stared ahead, stoic and blank as the class moved up the long flight of steps leading into the grim looking building.

"What's up with her?" Mallory whispered to Kyle. She had noticed Joyce's detached manner.

Still focused on nothing more than getting into the museum, Kyle shrugged. "Dunno."

Mallory's eyes narrowed. Joyce was a member of the Cedar Creek Junior High's elite *Fabulous Four*; a group of girls who tried to get Mallory to join their cliquey circle on her first day there. Unfortunately, by turning down their invitation, Mallory had committed an unforgivable sin in the minds of the somewhat spiteful Fabulous Four, and ever since, they had been relentless in trying to discover new ways to make her life miserable.

When the class entered the museum's foyer Mrs. Romano hurried over to the information booth. To one side loomed an enormous replica of an ancient Egyptian tomb fronted by fake stone pillars covered in mysterious looking hieroglyphics. Muted shades of amber and gold gave the impression that a hot desert sun was setting on an ancient burial crypt filled with kingly treasures.

As if he had been waiting for the group's arrival, a scholarly man with a wide smile hurried across the floor toward them. A tall severe-looking woman dressed in a long white toga scooted along beside him.

"Mrs. Romano, I presume?" the man said coming to a stop and reaching out to shake her hand. "My name is Silas Jarman, Head Curator here at Midville Museum." Glancing in the direction of the tomb entrance he lowered his voice as if reluctant to disturb the desert gloom. "I'm so glad you and your class could make it to our establishment today."

"We would like to thank you for giving us this wonderful opportunity," Mrs. Romano gushed. "And we're delighted to be here. Isn't that right, students?"

A collective "yes" echoed through the foyer. It seemed the students were unconcerned about disturbing the desert gloom.

"It's taken us over four years to get permission from the Egyptian Museum in Cairo for this display," Mr. Jarman said proudly, waving his hand in the direction of the exhibit. "It's on loan to us until–" He broke off realizing he had not introduced the toga-clad woman standing patiently beside him.

"Oh, dear, where are my manners. This is Miss Eleanor Snodgrass. She's one of our docents and will be your guide for the tour this afternoon."

At his introduction, Miss Snodgrass tugged a black Egyptian-style wig onto her head and turned to address the students. "Please feel free to ask questions as I lead you through the exhibit," she said with icy disdain. Then with little more than an annoyed sniff she spun on her thick-heeled shoes and strode toward the tomb entrance.

Mrs. Romano and the class followed, but as Mallory hastened through the monumental gateway, she was assailed by an overpowering smell of dust and mold. It left her with the strange feeling she had just stepped into a real underground tomb. Once through the entrance they passed columns of life-sized carved granite warriors and headed for the Egyptian wing. Miss Snodgrass then pointed out the ancient pottery shards and bronze vases in the lighted glass display cases. Overcome with the sudden increase in hot humid air, Mallory loosened her jacket, but soon bored with the docent's non-stop prattle about Egypt's musical instruments and odd-shaped oil lamps, she eventually wandered away.

Miss Snodgrass's dry, toneless voice followed. "Most of these items you see here today were discovered in royal tombs in the Valley of the Kings."

At the mention of the Valley of the Kings, Mallory felt a chill run down her neck. Annoyed at the museum's change in temperature, she buttoned up her coat again and rejoined the class as they followed Miss Snodgrass, oohing and aahing at all the displayed objects.

"Now I'm going to show you the highlight of our exhibit," she suddenly informed the class. With no further explanation she turned and made a beeline toward a small dimly lit room. After everyone had squeezed inside, Mallory looked around to see that the walls were softly painted with images of ancient Egyptian court life.

"This is what is called a sarcophagus," Miss Snodgrass said, pointing to a large alabaster container. Then, in an odd display of emotion, the docent's voice went breathless and reverent. "It was found in one of the royal tombs and contained three wooden coffins, one inside the other." She pointed to a brightly painted wooden coffin sitting roped off near the sarcophagus. "This is the smallest coffin, the one in which they found the body."

Everyone moved closer to peruse the mummy lying inside wrapped in an age-yellowed linen shroud. "You mean that's a real Pharaoh?" a student asked.

"It's a real mummy, but not a Pharaoh," explained Miss Snodgrass. "According to the hieroglyphics written on the outside of the coffin, it's the body of a young female temple singer called a muse."

"A muse is the name usually given to a woman who performs sacred music," Mrs. Romano added with a smile.

"Yes, well," continued the docent after a stiff lipped pause, "even more curious to Egyptologists is why this singer, who was not related to any of the royal families, was given such an elaborate burial by a prince of this dynasty."

The room fell silent as everyone continued to stare curiously into the coffin.

"Didn't they also refer to some singers as chantresses?" Kyle looked up to ask.

Miss Snodgrass turned to him, surprised. "Why, yes, they did."

Chalk one up for Kyle, Mallory thought as she loosened her jacket. The heat had returned.

"Please make a note, students, that hieroglyphs is a Greek word meaning *Sacred Carvings*," Miss Romano said. "It was one of the written languages used in ancient Egypt."

Miss Snodgrass sniffed indifferently and waited until she had everyone's attention again. "This particular mummy was, among other things, a harp player," she said. "And we know this because of the drawings on the outside of the sarcophagus. Musicians of that time also played flutes, bells, drums and castanets."

The lid to the wooden coffin stood propped up against the

sarcophagus and Mallory walked over to stare fascinated at the brightly painted female face carved upon it. The muse wore a dark wig and a neck collar encrusted with precious stones. Her deep blue eyes, outlined in heavy black kohl, stared back expressionless. "You're saying that mummy is the actual singer?" Mallory asked.

Miss Snodgrass nodded and pointed to a nearby photo showing the three original coffins. At that moment a gust of chilly air swept around Mallory.

"I wish they'd make up their mind with that darn air conditioning," she mumbled, turning to Kyle who joined her at that moment. "First I'm burning up, then I'm freezing."

Kyle shook his head, puzzled. "The temperature feels fine to me. You must be coming down with something." He left to study the statue of a long-eared dog sitting on a wooden shrine.

"That's the jackal god Anubis," Miss Romano called out, noting Kyle's interest. "The Egyptians believed he was one of the gods who ruled the Underworld. Isn't that correct, Miss Snodgrass?"

The docent nodded but looked annoyed.

Uncomfortable in the small airless room with its dank moldy odor, Mallory decided to move on. But when she turned to leave she came face-to-face with a coppery-skinned man dressed in a white linen wrap and leather-thonged sandals. Light bounced from his bronze helmet as he stepped forward, his face fierce and anxious. Saying nothing, he lifted his arm and pointed to the sarcophagus.

"Yeah, I saw it already," Mallory mumbled. She tried to bypass him, but he determinedly sidestepped her each time. Finally she darted under his arm and dashed from the room.

"Did you see that creepy-looking guard?" she asked Kyle when he joined her a moment later. "It was like he didn't want me to leave that room."

Kyle glanced around, but there was no sign of anyone. "How do you know he was a guard?"

"He acted like a guard," Mallory snorted, still irritated at the man's aggressiveness. "Plus he was wearing a costume like all the other people working here."

The class joined them at that moment and because their tour was nearing its end, Mrs. Romano gave everyone permission to wander around on their own. "And don't forget," she reminded them, "take lots of notes because we'll be discussing our trip in class tomorrow."

Twenty minutes later, the students were lined up back in the foyer ready to march out the door and down to their bus. Suddenly to everyone's surprise the floor began to shudder. Within seconds the jolting grew stronger and objects toppled from the display tables. Eleanor Snodgrass lurched from the tomb entrance tugging confusedly at her wig, her eyes wide in panic as a loud roar echoed through the museum.

"What's happening!" someone screamed.

"Make it stop!"

But the shaking grew even more violent.

Silas Jarman, the Head Curator, staggered into the foyer his face pale with shock. He teetered forward shouting, "Get down everyone! We're having an earthquake!"

Mrs. Romano's commanding voice rose above the increasing noise. "Students! Drop, cover and hold on."

Kyle grabbed Mallory and yanked her to the floor. The ceiling lamps swung overhead and doors slammed in the distance as heavy framed paintings slipped sideways on the walls.

And still the tremors continued.

"Is it really an earthquake?" Mallory gasped. The museum lamps flickered on and off and plaster dust rose up around them.

"I-I don't know," Kyle stammered, rolling out of the way of a stanchion crashing to the floor beside him. "Maybe we should make a run for it."

"No, it's not safe," Mr. Jarman cried. "Stay where you are."

And then, as quickly as it had started, the violent shuddering stopped.

An eerie silence swept through the museum.

"Is it over?" a voice whispered.

"There may be aftershocks," Mr. Jarman said. "Don't move until we know for sure."

Ignoring the warning, Miss Eleanor Snodgrass stumbled to her feet. Her toga had slipped off one shoulder and her wig sat lopsided on her head as she stared dazed at the mess around her.

Mr. Jarman waited a minute then rose to his feet, his face pallid. "I think we can all get up now."

The students rose slowly. Two of the girls sobbed quietly, scared and bewildered.

"Is everyone okay?" the head curator asked.

A few shaken voices murmured, "Yes," but the rest stayed silent.

Someone helped Mrs. Romano to her feet. She brushed herself off then instructed the class to exit the museum. "Go down and board the school bus," she said quietly. "I'll be right there."

The students filed silently through the front doors and down the steps.

Mrs. Romano turned to address the man beside her. "Thank you, Mr. Jarman," she said, her voice shaky. "I'll be in touch with you after I get the students safely back to Cedar Creek."

Mr. Jarman nodded absently.

After the class was seated back on the bus, Mrs. Romano instructed the driver to leave, post haste. Quiet to this point, Kyle whispered to Mallory. "I'm starting to think Midville is one heck of a dangerous place."

Mallory didn't answer. She was staring curiously out the window. "Kyle, check out those people walking along the street. They don't seem at all bothered by the earthquake. It's like they never even felt it."

Kyle frowned. "Yeah, it does seem strange," he murmured, his eyes narrow and curious.

Before either of them could comment further, the bus jolted into gear and took off. It chugged down the hill and veered quickly onto the main highway.

"I swear my knees are still shaking," Kyle whispered.

Mallory nodded slowly. It seemed 1977 was turning out to be

as strange as the year before. The farther the bus got from the museum, the louder the voices floated up from the back, each one more boastful than the previous.

"Yup, gotta admit. That was the best field trip I ever took."

"And I thought it was going to be boring."

"Did you see all those statues jiggling around on the table?"

"That was the coolest."

"Earthquakes don't scare me."

"Yeah, so how come you looked like you were crying?"

"I wasn't crying. I had dust in my eyes!"

Mallory shook her head in disgust.

Boys. Honestly.

Mrs. Romano did not relax until her students were seated safely back in their homeroom. "Well, I must say, our trip to the museum turned out to be more of an adventure than originally planned, didn't it?" she said, her eyes still holding the shadow of disbelief at what had happened.

A murmur of agreement swept through the room.

"The dismissal bell is about to ring," she continued, "so we won't be able to discuss what happened in Midville, however, we will definitely talk more about it in the coming days." She paused before adding. "I'll set it up with our school counselors to speak with anyone who needs help in processing what we've just been through, so please don't hesitate to let me know."

A few hands shot up. Mrs. Romano nodded.

"Yes, I know what you're going to ask, and yes, I still expect you to write a field report about the exhibit." She paused before adding, "You may also mention the earthquake, but no more than half a page about it. And don't forget, I'll need your papers by the end of the week."

After school let out, Mallory grabbed her bicycle and hurried over to the local park to get the dates and times for the start of the season's baseball practice. Eager to tell her grandmother about their experience at the museum, she was soon on the main street cycling past the pink striped ice cream shop and Mr. Harmon's antique store. When she reached *Ye Olde Tea Shoppe,* she wheeled her bicycle up the side alley and hurried in through the back door of her grandmother's cozy tearoom.

"Aggie?" she called as the door slammed shut behind her. "You'll never believe what just happened at–"

Mallory came to a sudden stop. The warm homey teashop, smelling of fresh-baked pastries, appeared to be empty.

"Aggie?"

"Yo," came a voice as her grandmother, clutching a large tray, backed out of her over-sized pantry. "What's the emergency?"

Mallory hurried to help with the heavy platter. "You'll never believe what I've just been through."

"Bet I can," Aggie said. She slid the croissants and Danish pastries onto a shelf beneath the counter then straightened up. "An earthquake, right?" Her grin was sly as she tucked a strand of henna-colored hair under her comb.

"How could you possibly know that?"

"Well, I could try to fool you and say I've finally developed some psychic abilities, but you probably wouldn't believe me anyway, so here's the truth."

Aggie said nothing more until she had handed Mallory a steaming hot cup of mango-peach tea, filled a plate with cream puff pastries, and with a second cup of tea, led the way to a comfortable table.

"Joyce Danner was just in here." Aggie said, pulling out a chair and beckoning Mallory to sit.

"Joyce! Here? Why?"

"To get one of your detective cards, that's how I know what happened at Midville."

Mallory paused in the process of reaching for a pasty. After their last mystery, she had decided to go into the business of solving crimes and had designed some business cards for it. But to her knowledge this was the first time anyone had actually taken one.

"By the way, you forgot to put your phone number on the cards so I had to tell her what it was. Hope that was okay."

"Sure." Mallory jumped up to retrieve the stack of cards sitting at the end of the counter in a hand-shaped holder. Returning to the table she grabbed a pen and started writing the phone number on each card.

"Here's what I bet you don't know," Aggie continued, scooping two teaspoons of sugar into her teacup and stirring it with the speed of an arthritic snail.

Mallory sat back. This could take a while. Her grandmother loved keeping people in suspense.

"Take a guess," Aggie eventually said.

"Aggie, I've been through a very frightening experience. I don't want to take a guess."

"Okay, if you insist," Aggie answered curtly. "You know, of course, that Joyce's mother is a curator at the museum. She wasn't there today, but according to Joyce she apparently found out that the shaking you all felt only happened on the first floor."

Mallory stared at her grandmother puzzled. "That doesn't make any sense."

"The museum authorities decided it was probably due to an underground gas explosion."

Mallory snorted in disbelief. "More like someone was either trying to get our attention or stop us from leaving the museum."

"Hmm, that's a novel thought," Aggie pondered. "Any idea who?"

Mallory shook her head. "Did Joyce say why she wanted my card?"

"No. Looked like she'd been crying. I didn't want to question her."

Mallory remembered earlier that day how glum Joyce had been when Mrs. Romano reminded the class to thank her mother for the field trip. "There's something odd going on here, Aggie," Mallory said. "What we went through couldn't have been a gas explosion, especially if it only affected the first floor. It started slowly and pretty soon everything was swaying and all kinds of things were toppling over. If it were a gas explosion, there wouldn't be all that shaking and rolling stuff going on, would there?"

"I wouldn't think so, but I've never experienced a gas explosion, or for that matter, an earthquake," Aggie replied, "But logic tells me a gas explosion would be like one big sudden bang."

Mallory's frown deepened. "Wait until Kyle hears what those museum people are saying."

The bell over the door announced the unexpected arrival of Kyle himself. Aggie and Mallory watched silently as he strode over, pulled off his jacket, and threw it carelessly across the back of an empty chair.

"Wait until Kyle hears what?" he said, slumping heavily onto the nearest seat.

"Nothing wrong with your ears," Aggie grunted.

Mallory turned to Kyle. "Aggie just found out that the earthquake at the museum was not an earthquake, but a gas explosion that only affected the first floor."

"No way."

"No way that's hard to believe, or no way it wasn't an

explosion?" Mallory asked.

Kyle shook his head vehemently. "No way it was an explosion."

Mallory nodded in agreement. "That's what I think, too."

"Any clues on what it was then, Kyle?" asked Aggie.

"Somebody had a bean burrito for lunch?"

"Get serious," Mallory snapped. Aggie struggled not to laugh.

"Mr. Jarman called it an earthquake," Kyle said. "And the way everything was shaking, I would have thought the whole city was feeling it. I can't believe it was only felt in the museum."

"Still it would explain why those people on the street were so unconcerned," Mallory said.

Kyle reached for a pastry. "I wonder why the museum is saying it wasn't an earthquake?"

Aggie turned to Mallory. "Did you tell Kyle your thoughts on what happened at the museum?"

"No. I'm still working on that idea," Mallory said.

At that moment the bell over the door tinkled again. Aggie stood to greet the two women who stepped inside. "I think you two may have a mystery on your hands," she called back, as she headed off to serve her customers.

"Working on what idea?" Kyle asked, stuffing the last piece of pastry in his mouth.

Mallory leaned over to whisper, "I don't think we went through an explosion or an earthquake. I think someone was trying to get our attention."

"Someone like who?"

"I didn't tell you this before, but when we left that room with the mummy–"

Kyle gave a strangled groan. "Are you sure I want to hear this?"

"Yes, you do," Mallory frowned before continuing. "I saw that big dog statue–"

Kyle rolled his eyes. "Anubis, the jackal god, yeah, I know the one."

"It was staring at me."

"That statue looks like it's staring at everybody."

"Well, this was different."

"In what way different?"

"Its eyes glinted bright yellow . . ."

Kyle swallowed hard. He had a feeling he was about to hear more.

" . . . then they blinked at me. Twice."

The following day at school, Mallory hurried into the lunch
area. She saw Kyle reading at his favorite tree-shaded table
and headed toward him.

"Hey, Mallory, seen any good ghosts lately?" a voice called
behind her. It was Sarah, one of the Fabulous Four girls. They were
all seated at a table smirking in her direction.

"No," Mallory called back, "but if I do, I'll be sure to have
them get in touch with you." She continued on across the
compound and a moment later slid onto the bench opposite Kyle.

"Thanks to you, I didn't sleep much last night," Kyle said, his
head still down reading his book.

"Me? Why?" Mallory pulled out her lunch and spread it on
the table.

"I kept having this nightmare where I was being chased by a
long-eared dachshund wearing a pharaoh's wig."

Mallory giggled. "No kidding. Did the dachshund catch
you?"

Kyle looked up. "Not funny, Mallory. I was so tired I couldn't
focus in science class this morning."

Mallory stifled another laugh then looked up as a shadow fell
across the table. Joyce Danner, who had been sitting with the

Fabulous Four a moment earlier, now stood beside her.

"Sorry to interrupt," Joyce said, her voice low, "but I really need to talk to you." She bit the inside of her lip before glancing uncomfortably back at her group. They had stopped eating, staring over at her in surprise.

"Sure," said Mallory, sliding to the end of the bench to make room.

Joyce glanced uncertainly at Kyle.

"Kyle's all right," Mallory said. "He's my partner, so whatever you say he'll get to hear about anyway."

With a resigned shrug, Joyce squeezed in beside Mallory. "Your grandma probably told you I picked up one of your detective cards yesterday," she said.

"Yup, she sure did."

Joyce leaned forward, her voice little more than a whisper. "It's about my mother," she said. "She's a curator at the Midville Museum—"

"Talking about that museum," Kyle interrupted, "did we go through an earthquake there yesterday or not?"

Joyce played nervously with the buttons on her blouse. "The museum officials are telling everyone it was either a gas explosion, or the foundation shifted."

"That doesn't sound right," Kyle said.

"The engineers are checking on it today," Joyce said.

Mallory narrowed her eyes at Joyce. "But you don't believe what the museum is saying?"

"I don't. Nor does my mother."

"So, what do you and your mother think it was?" asked Kyle.

"An earthquake," Joyce replied without hesitation.

"An earthquake that only happened on the lower floor?" Mallory asked incredulously.

Joyce nodded. "And the earthquake is not the first strange thing that's happened at the museum." Joyce shuffled her feet uneasily before glancing back over her shoulder. "I'd rather not say anything more about it here, though."

Kyle leaned forward, his tiredness gone. "Let's meet in Aggie's teashop after school," he whispered. "We can talk there."

"That would be good," nodded Joyce. She stood to return to her table, and then looked back. "I've been wanting to say for a long time that I'm really sorry about how I treated you when you first came to this school, Mallory. I know you didn't want to be a part of our group and I wish I could have done what you did and just have walked away." She sighed deeply before striding away to rejoin the Fab Four.

Maureen, Renee, and Sarah leaned forward to ask her questions, but Joyce simply picked up her sandwich and resumed eating leaving them glaring surly and frustrated at her silence.

Mallory and Kyle were already seated at *Ye Olde Tea Shoppe* when Joyce arrived later that afternoon. At the sound of the doorbell, Aggie looked up from behind the counter where she stood measuring loose tea for a waiting customer. She waved to Joyce as she crossed the floor to join Mallory and Kyle.

"Thanks for meeting me," Joyce said, sitting down. She sounded breathless and scared and rubbed her hand wearily across her forehead before continuing. "The museum is letting my mother go."

"Your mother's going to be fired?" Kyle gasped.

"No, laid off," Joyce corrected. "The museum says it's having budget problems and has to downsize, but there's strange stuff going on there and I think that docent, Miss Sour Face Snodgrass is behind it all."

Joyce stopped talking as the door tinkled musically and the customer departed. Quick as a bunny, Aggie scurried across the floor to join them.

"Joyce, can I get you a cup of tea or coffee, dear?" she asked.

"No, thank you, Mrs. Hobbs." Joyce glanced at Mallory, uncertain.

"Oh, don't worry about Aggie, either," Mallory said, flashing a grin in her grandmother's direction. "Sooner or later she'll find out what's going on so we may as well include her now and get it over and done with."

Aggie glared at her granddaughter before pulling out a chair and sitting down. "Okay, I'm all ears," she said, turning to Joyce. "What's going on?"

"Joyce's mother is about to be laid off from the museum," Kyle said.

Aggie reared back, horrified. "Laid off? But she's an excellent curator. Has been for years. What brought this on?"

Joyce fingered the tablecloth, scrunching it up and smoothing it out a number of times before replying. "The Head Curator, Mr. Jarman, decided he had to let some people go. My mother is one. On top of that, some important items are missing."

"Don't tell me he thinks your mother has something to do with that?" Aggie gasped.

"No, but someone is making accusations against her."

"Accusations! Poppycock!" Aggie sputtered. "Your mother is as honest as the day is long. Who's making up these stories?"

"She doesn't know."

Mallory waited until Aggie calmed down before asking Joyce, "What makes you think Miss Snodgrass is involved?"

Joyce looked disgusted. "Mr. Claxley hired her a few months ago and ever since she's been trying to make Mom look bad."

"And Mr. Claxley is . . . ?" Mallory asked.

"The assistant curator at the museum. His first name is Mortimus."

"And Miss Snodgrass," Aggie asked. "Who is she?"

"One of the docents who works there," Mallory said, turning to her grandmother.

"Her full name is Eleanor Snodgrass and she's a really strange woman," Joyce added. "She's also thick as thieves with Mr. Claxley. That's why I think they're plotting something."

"Hmm," Aggie murmured thoughtfully.

Mallory turned to Aggie. "We need to know the full story before we make any assumptions about who's behind what, Aggie."

"What? Who? Me?" Aggie spluttered. "I haven't made a single assumption so far. Why the look?"

Mallory shrugged at her grandmother. "Well, you usually . . . "

Aggie ignored the comment and reached for Joyce's hand. She gave it a comforting squeeze. "Now, don't you worry, Mallory and Kyle will figure this thing out. I guarantee you that."

"Well, we haven't agreed to–" Mallory began.

Kyle interrupted. "If Mal and I were to help, would your mother tell us more about what's going on?"

Joyce gave a helpless shrug. "Well, she wasn't too happy when I told her I wanted to talk to you about everything . . . she likes you and all, it's just that–" Joyce broke off, then added, "If you would help then maybe I could convince her to tell you more."

She glanced at her watch and jumped to her feet. "Sorry, I have to get back," she said, pushing a scrunched up piece of paper toward them. "Here's our phone number." She headed toward the door then looked back. "You might find it hard to believe all the weird stuff that's been happening at the museum," she frowned.

"Probably not," Aggie called back. "In fact, the weirder it is, the more we'll probably believe it."

The bell tinkled and the door slammed shut as a puzzled Joyce stepped through to the outside. Aggie turned to Kyle. "You've got to admit," she said, "life was certainly dull and boring in Cedar Creek before Mallory arrived, wasn't it?"

Kyle sighed. "And before Mallory arrived my parents believed I was going to be an astrophysicist. Now they think I'm heading for a life of crime."

Mallory grinned. "Guess that's the price for solving other people's problems."

"Get any feelings about what Joyce was saying?" Aggie turned to ask Mallory.

"No. But obviously something isn't right at the museum––" Mallory stopped abruptly to look at Kyle who was staring intently at something behind her.

"What are you looking at, Kyle?" she asked.

He pointed to the floor. "Don't you think that's odd?"

Both Aggie and Mallory followed his gaze.

"You mean that shadow?" Aggie asked.

Kyle nodded.

"Not really," Aggie shrugged. "The sun creates shadows in here every afternoon."

"But look at the shape of that particular one."

Aggie leaned closer. "Hmm, you're right. It does look unusual."

"Unusual? How?" Mallory frowned.

"It's shaped like an ankh," Kyle said. "The ancient Egyptian symbol for life."

Aggie peered closer at the shadowy cross with its rounded top. "Kyle's right," she said excited. "It's like you're getting a message from beyond."

Mallory shook her head—her grandmother was always looking for the supernatural angle in everything. "Why can't I just have a normal crime to solve instead of a *woo woo* mystery?" she sighed.

"I don't know, granddaughter," Aggie said, "but you shouldn't ignore this sign. I have a feeling it's important."

Mallory had agreed to help Aggie out the following day so after a quick breakfast she set off on her bike, deep in thought about Joyce and her strange request. A few early Saturday morning shoppers strolled along the thoroughfare as Mallory rode up Main Street toward the teashop.

When Aggie saw Mallory coming through the back door, she clapped her hands in relief. "Good, you're finally here. We have a lot to do today."

"Victoria said she'd come over later to help."

Aggie smiled. "Great, I can use the extra hands."

Victoria Carlson and her mother had moved into Marlatt Manor six months earlier, after Mallory and Kyle solved the mystery of who was trying to steal their family mansion. They had been good friends ever since.

"So who are you expecting this morning?" Mallory asked as she helped Aggie spread a white cloth on a large round table and set it with dainty porcelain cups and saucers.

"The D.O.S.R. ladies." Aggie grinned. She handed Mallory a centerpiece of freshly cut carnations. "The acronym stands for *Daughters of the Southern Republic.* They've decided to hold their monthly meetings in my tea shop."

"Daughters of the Southern Republic? Sounds like something from the Civil War."

"More like the great-granddaughters of the Civil War," Aggie said, smoothing the wrinkles from the tablecloth. "They're determined to keep the memory of their ancestors alive."

"Well, before they get here," Mallory said, "I want to talk to you about Mrs. Danner's problem."

Aggie glanced across at her granddaughter. "I'm listening, fire away."

"I don't think I'm the right one to help her," Mallory explained. She paused to place serviettes around the table.

"Why not?" Aggie asked, surprised.

Mallory shrugged. "Well, getting someone's job back isn't exactly what a crime detective does . . . is it?"

Aggie chewed thoughtfully on her bottom lip. "Perhaps, but I think there are some things you need to consider. First, if there's something supernatural going on at the museum, you know you're not going to be left alone until you do something about it, right?"

Malory's shoulders dropped. "And what's the second thing?" she sighed.

Aggie sat down and gestured for Mallory to do the same.

"The second thing," Aggie began, "is something I think you should be aware of before you make a final decision." She stopped and looked off sadly into the distance before continuing. "I've known Emily Danner for many years now. The Danner's have stayed quite private about their personal affairs, but in a small community like this, it's not hard to figure things out." Aggie took a deep troubled breath. "Let me see, if this is 1977, then it all started about nine years ago, in 1968. That's when Emily's husband was drafted into the army and sent overseas to fight in Vietnam. Three years later Emily was notified that Vietcong forces had captured him, and not long after that the War Office received word he had died in a prisoner-of-war camp." Aggie paused and her eyes moistened over. "It near to broke Emily's heart when she was notified of her husband's death, not to mention the big hole it left in Joyce's life losing her father at such a young age."

"I'm sorry," Mallory whispered. "I didn't know any of this."

"Well, how could you? No one likes to talk about that war much. In hindsight it really was such a wasteful one." Aggie looked down and shook her head. "Anyway, things were not easy for Emily after that. She struggled financially to raise her daughter and take care of her ailing father who was living with them at the time. Getting the curator's job at the museum was a God-send."

"Struggled?" Mallory frowned astonished. "I thought Joyce was one of the rich kids in town. She's part of that Fabulous Four group at school, you know."

"I know the group you're talking about," Aggie snorted, "but it doesn't mean a thing. Probably makes Joyce feel important to be hanging out with them. Can't think of any other reason why she'd do it." Aggie pursed her lips and studied Mallory thoughtfully. "Getting back to this present situation, though, I think Emily Danner is more upset about the rumors she's involved with a theft at the museum, than being laid off."

Mallory sat up straighter. "Hmm, a theft is definitely a crime needing to be solved, isn't it?" She reached into her pocket to retrieve the crumpled piece of paper Joyce had handed her.

"Does this mean Mallory Gilmartin, detective extraordinaire, is officially back on the job?" Aggie asked with a grin.

Mallory gave a firm nod.

Aggie slapped the table. "That's my girl," she beamed, as Mallory stared at Joyce's hastily scrawled phone number.

At that moment six elderly women bustled in through the

front door. One of the grey-haired women looked over and called out, her voice loud and shrill, "Afternoon, Aggie!"

Aggie sent a conspiratorial smile in Mallory's direction. "Wait for it. She's not done yet," she whispered.

The woman raised a fist above her head. "We're here to save the South!"

Aggie grinned and called back. "Of course you are, Esther. And the citizens of this great state of Virginia are blessed to have such a noble group working on their behalf."

The six women, all wearing red sashes embroidered with the letters **D.O.S.R.**, headed with delightful enthusiasm toward the reserved table.

Mallory hid her smile as she excused herself and walked over to the phone sitting on Aggie's counter. She dialed the Danner's number and after introducing herself to Joyce's mother, asked if she and Kyle might visit her later that afternoon. After she hung up, Mallory gave Aggie a 'thumbs up'.

It was noon by the time Kyle and Mallory left Aggie's teashop and headed through the woods toward the Danner's house. The day was sunny with pools of sunlight snaking across the dirt road ahead of them.

"Mrs. Danner said it was okay if we stopped by to see her, right?" Kyle called out, pedaling hard to keep up.

Mallory nodded.

Kyle squinted at her suspiciously, grumbling to himself about the sorry lack of communication between some partners in crime, but he said nothing more. Twenty minutes later they came to a small community of tract homes and Mallory slowed down so Kyle could catch up.

"I hate it when you race ahead like that," he beefed. "I can never ask you any questions."

"Exactly," Mallory smiled mischievously. "Anyway, you know where Joyce lives so lead the way."

Kyle rode ahead and after biking down a tree-lined avenue, turned onto a narrow lane. A moment later he pulled up outside a cream-colored house set back from the street. Mallory leaned her bike on the fence next to Kyle's and followed him up the path to the front porch.

Joyce appeared almost immediately. "Mom's waiting for you." She held the door open and motioned them through. They followed her into a bright yellow kitchen where Emily Danner stood leaning back against the breakfast counter. The petite woman, not much taller than her daughter, was dressed in a pair of tight black pants and a red oversized sweater. She studied their approach, her face impassive.

"Mom, this is Mallory Gilmartin and Kyle Johnson. They're both in my class at school," Joyce said.

Emily Danner smiled in greeting then gestured for everyone to sit at the table. She turned to reach into a cupboard for four drinking glasses. "I appreciate your offer to try and help sort all this out," she said over her shoulder, "but as I told Joyce, I doubt there's much anyone can do. The whole situation just seems to get stranger by the day."

"You have to tell them everything, Mother," Joyce said. "If they're going to help, they need to know all the details."

Mrs. Danner placed four glasses of soda on the table and sat down. "Well, I guess all this stuff at the museum began soon after the Egyptian exhibit arrived. That's when things got . . . well . . . rather creepy." She gazed absently at the moisture gathering on the outside of her drinking glass.

"Mrs. Danner, before you tell us anything, may I ask you some questions?" Mallory said.

"Yes, of course."

Mallory twisted her baseball cap sideways on her head, something she did whenever she was about to think deeply. She grabbed a pencil, and adopting her most serious detective voice, began, "Is it true the museum is laying you off from your job?"

"Yes."

"Why?"

"According to Mr. Jarman, the budget for the museum was less this year because the benefactors' contributions were not as generous as they had been in the past. This has forced the museum to cut corners."

While Mallory scribbled furiously in her notebook, Kyle asked, "But didn't the museum just hire a new docent?"

"You mean Eleanor Snodgrass? Well, it's understandable. She's knowledgeable in Egyptian history, and they needed more docents for the exhibit."

Mallory looked up and frowned. "Even though they were trying to cut corners?"

"That's exactly what I thought," Joyce chimed in. She spoke directly to Mallory. "Personally, I think Miss *Nose-In-The-Air* Snodgrass is after Mother's job."

Mrs. Danner shook her head. "We don't really know that, Joyce."

Judging by her clamped lips, Joyce wasn't about to be swayed from her opinion.

Mallory nodded thoughtfully then jotted down more notes. "Could there be any other reason why they're letting you go, Mrs. Danner?" she asked.

"Yes, I believe so," came the woman's swift reply. "You see there are some items that have gone missing from the museum and it seems I'm under suspicion for their disappearance. Believe me when I say I've not taken anything, but in thinking back, I realize this rumor began shortly after I witnessed a particularly odd incident there."

"Is this the *creepy* part you mentioned earlier?" Kyle asked.

Emily Danner didn't answer. She simply stood, hurried over to the window and after slamming it closed and locking it tight, rejoined the three curious teenagers.

"Can't be too sure who might be listening," she shrugged before continuing. "Well, when the Egyptian exhibit arrived at the museum most of the staff volunteered to work a number of late nights to help set it up." Mrs. Danner stopped and took a deep breath.

"It's okay, Mother." Joyce placed her hand gently on her mother's arm.

Kyle watched in surprise at this display of affection from the usually stoic and emotionless girl.

"Most everyone had gone home on this particular night," Emily Danner continued. "I was about to leave when I thought I heard a noise coming from the basement. I thought it strange that anyone would be down there at that hour so I went searching for the night security guard the museum had hired to watch over the exhibit. When I couldn't find him, I thought I'd better go check it out for myself. When I stepped into the basement there was a strong smell of incense and a lamp flickering on a workbench. Two shadowy figures in hooded cloaks were standing behind it, and one was chanting something in a language I'd never heard before."

"No kidding!" Kyle exclaimed. His glasses had slipped down his nose in excitement.

"The person chanting raised his arms. I could see an odd green light reflecting off his cloak and I had the impression he was in some kind of a trance."

"Mother," Joyce gasped, "you never told me this part!"

Emily Danner shrugged apologetically at her daughter before turning back to Mallory and Kyle. "I know it all sounds rather unbelievable, but trust me, I know what I saw that night."

"Did you know who these two people were?" Mallory asked.

"Not at first." Emily Danner stopped and twirled the straw in her soda.

"The person chanting appeared to be reading from a large book open in front of him. He must have heard me step into the basement because the noise snapped him out of his trance. When he looked up I could see it was Mortimus Claxley. He started yelling and accusing me of spying on him. His face was so full of rage it truly frightened me, and he demanded I leave immediately."

"Mortimus Claxley, the curator at the museum, right?" Kyle asked.

"Yes, Mr. Jarman's right-hand man, I guess you could say," Joyce's mother replied. "He's considered an asset to the museum because he's skilled in educational programs and exhibit design."

"Did you see who the other person was?" Mallory asked.

"No, they were standing in the shadows and I couldn't make them out."

Mallory's pencil scratching furiously in her notebook filled the silence in the room. "Did Mr. Claxley ever tell you later what he was doing in the basement that night?" she leaned forward to ask.

"No, and after that he began to find fault with everything I did."

Joyce broke in. "Meantime he's convinced Mr. Jarman that my mother is probably responsible for the items missing from the museum."

"It's more like he *inferred* I might have something to do with it," Joyce's mother said.

"And did all this weird stuff happen before or after Mr. Claxley hired Eleanor Snodgrass?" Mallory asked.

Emily Danner looked up, surprised. "I'm pretty sure it was after he hired her. But there were other weird things that started happening at the museum."

Kyle ran his fingers through his curly hair and blinked

rapidly. "Weird things? Like what?"

The trio waited expectantly as Mrs. Danner continued. "Every morning, soon after the arrival of the exhibit, we would find one of our ushabti statues facing backward on the shelf where we had placed it."

"Ushabti?" Mallory asked, puzzled.

"Yes, an ushabti is a statue the ancient Egyptians carved and buried in their tombs with the dead. This particular ushabti was about twelve inches high."

"Did this statue come with the exhibit?" Mallory asked.

"No, even though there were a number of them that did come with the exhibit, this particular one belonged to the Midville Museum," continued Mrs. Danner. "At first we thought someone was playing a joke on us, but after Mr. Jarman locked the statue up in a glass case and hid the key–the only key I might add–he would find the figurine turned around when he got to his office the next day. In the end he hid it."

"Do you know where?" Mallory asked.

Mrs. Danner shrugged. "No, I don't, and after things started going missing in the museum, I guess I forgot about it."

"If Mr. Jarman thinks you might have something to do with these thefts, why are you still working there?" Mallory asked.

Emily Danner shook her head. "I wanted to leave, but because they needed all the staff they could get for the exhibit, and because there was no real proof I had anything to do with the thefts, they asked me to stay until it was over. I decided it wouldn't be fair to everyone else if I left, so I agreed to the arrangement."

"And when will that arrangement end?" Kyle asked.

"In about a week and a half."

"That's when your job ends?" Mallory reiterated.

"Correct. That's when the exhibit will be packed up and

returned to the museum in Cairo."

Mallory scribbled more notes then looked up. "Besides the statue turning around and Mr. Claxley acting all weird-like, is there anything else going on?"

Mrs. Danner frowned before answering. "Well, now that I think about it, yes. Soon after we set up the Egyptian artifacts for display, I kept seeing a light coming from the room where we displayed the mummy, but when I'd go in there, I wouldn't find anything to account for it."

"The mummy room?" Kyle gasped. "That's where–" he stopped short. Mallory had kicked him under the table.

Joyce swung around to stare at him. "Where what?"

"Where we learned that other people beside pharaohs have been buried in royal tombs," Mallory said quickly.

Mrs. Danner gave a half smile. "Yes, that particular mummy is quite a mystery to Egyptologists. They still haven't figured out why a temple singer was buried in a royal chamber."

Mallory took a sip from her soda. "Mrs. Danner, we don't have school Monday because of a teacher's conference. Could you get Kyle and me into the museum so we can check things out?"

Kyle threw Mallory a look, but she ignored him.

"Yes, of course, I don't think that should be a problem," Emily Danner nodded. "They've closed the museum for a couple of days to check things out, but I believe it should be open by Monday. I'll call you that morning if there's a problem, otherwise I'll leave two tickets at the Will Call window. Keep in mind, though, that the museum closes at four-thirty each afternoon so you'll need to leave by then."

"How are you going to get to Midville?" Joyce asked.

"We'll ride our bikes," Mallory said. "It shouldn't take us more than forty-five minutes, right?" she turned to ask Kyle.

"Y-y-yeah, sure." Kyle stared suspiciously. Mallory was up to something, and whatever it was, he was about to be dragged smack-dab right into the middle of it.

Mallory turned back to Joyce's mother. "How many security guards work at the museum?"

"We have a regular day guard who goes home after the museum closes, and then a night guard, the one who was hired to watch the exhibit."

Mallory wrote hastily. "And where is Mr. Jarman's office?"

Mrs. Danner looked puzzled. "It's next to mine on the first floor–along the corridor with the rest of the administrative offices."

"Do they lock the offices at night?" Mallory asked casually.

Mrs. Danner shook her head. "I don't believe they do," she replied.

"And the basement? Mallory asked.

"No. That I know for sure. It hasn't been locked in years.

Mallory stood and gave a quick thank you, indicating she and Kyle would let themselves out. She waved goodbye to Joyce and hastened from the kitchen.

"Thanks for the sodas," Kyle called and followed Mallory out the door. Whatever she was up to, he knew he was not going to like it.

Mallory rode silently alongside Kyle back into the woods. She was still thinking about the incredible story they'd just heard from Emily Danner.

"We need to talk to Aggie," Mallory finally said.

Kyle glanced over. Mallory's baseball hat was twisted to one side, yet he had distinctly remembered seeing her pull it forward before they left the Danner's house. "Okay Mallory, what is going on in that devious mind of yours? I know you're planning something."

"Me?" Mallory turned with an exaggerated look of innocence. "You think I'm planning something?"

Kyle stopped. "I know you are. And I'm not moving until you tell me why we're going to Midville on Monday."

Mallory stopped beside him. "To visit the museum."

"And . . .?"

Mallory straightened her cap and raced past the dense growth of pine trees and thick ferns.

"Listen Mal," Kyle said catching up, "I'm not going with you Monday unless you tell me what's going on."

A lone woodpecker rapped in the distance as if it, too, demanded an answer.

Mallory slowed down. "Okay, here it is," she said. "We, as in you and I, are going to the museum. And we, as in you and I, are going to hide inside the museum after it closes."

"No way!" Kyle said, puffing from his fast ride.

"Kyle, something is going on in that museum and this may be our only chance to find out what it is before that exhibit goes back to Egypt."

Mallory sped off again.

Kyle groaned. I should've left town when I had the chance, he thought. Right after we solved the mystery of Miss Florentine's missing Ming vase.

It was late in the afternoon when Mallory and Kyle reached Aggie's small cottage. They hurried through the glass-beaded curtain separating the hall from the kitchen to find Aggie sitting at the table waiting. Beside her sat Mallory's fifteen-year-old older brother Ron and her friend Victoria.

"Figured you'd eventually check in at headquarters so I called in the rest of the team," Aggie said, gesturing toward Ron and Victoria. "Now sit down and tell us what you learned at Emily Danner's."

Mallory scooted next to Aggie on the bench seat. "You won't believe what's going on in the Midville Museum," she said, reaching for her notebook.

"I'll second that," Kyle said, wiping the perspiration from his brow as he sat down beside her.

Aggie's tabby cat, Smothers, hearing Mallory's voice, jumped down from the overhead shelf where he had been stretched out fast asleep and climbed lazily into her lap. Mallory leaned over to whisper in his ear. "Hey, Smothers, I just found out Bastet is the Egyptian goddess of cats. If I happen to run into her, I'll put in a good word for you. Promise."

The cat gave a wide yawn of disinterest and promptly fell back to sleep.

After skimming her notes Mallory relayed everything Mrs. Danner had told them, including the story about the items missing from the museum.

"So that's the theft Emily Danner is being accused of?" Aggie said.

"Not accused, but under suspicion," Kyle corrected.

"That's just as bad," Aggie retorted.

Ron turned to Mallory. "Do you think the basement business she stumbled upon is connected to the exhibit?" he asked.

"Yeah, I think that's pretty obvious," Mallory said.

"Then perhaps Claxley was in the middle of conjuring up some kind of ancient spell or curse when Mrs. Danner disturbed him," Ron added.

Everyone waited curiously for him to continue.

"From what I've read," he explained, "the ancient Egyptian kings and queens believed that when they died they would pass into a place called the afterlife where they would continue to rule. Their bodies were prepared extensively for this journey in a series of funerary rituals, and because they believed in magic, they used a lot of spells and curses to ward off any evil they might encounter along the way."

"Even if he could, why would Mr. Claxley be conjuring up a spell or curse?" Mallory asked.

In the silence that settled between them it was obvious no one had an answer.

"I have books you can read," Ron finally turned to Mallory.

"Thanks," she said, cringing at the thought of studying any history books.

"We had an assignment on ancient Egypt in my last school," Victoria said. "I read that the really great stuff in the tombs was stolen by grave robbers years before the first archeologists arrived. It wasn't until they found King Tut's untouched tomb that they realized how much had probably been stolen from all the other grave sites."

Mallory frowned. It seemed everybody knew a whole lot more about ancient Egypt than she did—with the exception of Aggie of course, whose face wore the same astonished look as her own.

"Oh, and there's another strange thing that happened while Kyle and I were at the Danner's," Mallory said, glancing down at her notes. "When Mrs. Danner was telling us about what happened in the basement, I thought I saw a white mist appear in their kitchen."

"You didn't mention that after we left the Danner's house!" Kyle cried.

"That's because I didn't know what it was. Still don't," Mallory mumbled. "But it did give me an odd feeling."

"Like what?" Aggie frowned.

"Like someone was listening to us." Mallory closed her notebook and stuffed it back in her bag. "So, here's what Kyle and I are going to do Monday," she announced. "We're going to the museum and when they close at four-thirty–"

"You'll hide there," Aggie said with a grin as Kyle moaned out loud. "Well, it's what I'd do."

Mallory grinned back at her grandmother. They had often been accused of thinking alike.

"In fact, I'll go with you," Aggie added. "I can drive the get-away car."

Oblivious to Mallory's sudden grimace, Aggie continued

with her plan to join them at the museum. "I'll get Martha Deacon to take over the teashop for the afternoon. She's helped out before and loves doing it."

"Good idea," Victoria said. "Mom and I are going out of town for the long weekend and we won't need Mrs. Deacon to do any cooking for us. I'm sure she'd be available."

Mallory groaned inwardly. Aggie's psychedelic painted van would stand out like a sore thumb, especially after hours.

"Aggie, I think it would be much easier if Kyle and I went alone. Your VW is not only noisy, but it's way too identifiable with all those symbols painted over it. We can hide our bikes in the bushes and get away faster if we have to," Mallory said.

"She's got a point there," Kyle agreed.

"You're probably right," Aggie sighed, disappointed. "But watch out the next time you need a ride in my noisy old van."

At that everyone laughed and stood to leave.

Aggie accompanied them to the door and wished them goodbye. As the teenagers followed each other up the path, Smothers, now fully awake, squeezed past Aggie's legs, attempting to waddle out after them.

"Oh, no you don't," she muttered, bending down to grab him. "You stay here. I need someone to help me figure out a backup plan."

Chapter 7

When Mallory got home, she leaned her bicycle against the wall and ran up the steps onto the porch. "I'm back!" she called.

The house was filled with the delicious aroma of baking meat loaf so Mallory headed to the kitchen. There she found her mother gazing into space with a wide excited smile.

"What's up with all the happiness, Mom?"

Lorna removed the dish from the oven and placed it on top of the stove. She wiped her hands on her apron then turned to Mallory with a grin. "Kevin Mason just called. He flew in to see his grandmother this weekend and wants me to go out to dinner with him tomorrow night. Of course, I said '*yes*', she smiled shyly.

"Of course," Mallory repeated, but her stomach lurched.

Kevin was an architect who lived in Boston. He had helped Mallory and Kyle with their recent Ming vase mystery, and after his grandmother came to Cedar Creek to live with her cousin, Edna May Florentine, Kevin promised to visit as often as possible. This was his first time back since Aggie had opened her teashop. But the idea of a suitor going after her mother fell like a dead fly in Mallory's ointment of hope that her parents might one day reunite.

Her thoughts were interrupted as Ron strolled into the

kitchen carrying three large books. He deposited them with a thump on the table. "Here are the books on ancient Egypt I was telling you about. I checked them out of the local public library a few days ago. Thought you might want to take a look at them before they're due back."

"Thanks," Mallory said, still distracted by her mother's news.

If Ron was aware of Kevin coming to Cedar Creek, he certainly didn't appear to be bothered by it. And this annoyed Mallory even more. She grabbed the three heavy volumes and marched up the stairs to her room deciding that she and Ron needed a united front concerning their mother's future. Once inside, Mallory dropped the books on the bedside table and reached for the phone.

"Aggie, something awful has happened!" she said, barely giving her grandmother a chance to say hello.

"Good Lord, child, what's wrong?"

"Kevin Mason came to visit his grandmother this weekend."

Mallory paused, waiting for Aggie to say something, but she didn't.

"Aggie?" Even a gasp would have been better than nothing, for heaven's sake.

"I'm here. I'm just trying to figure out what the *awful* part of that news is."

"He's taking Mom out to dinner tomorrow night!"

Again there was a long pause.

"And?" Aggie finally asked.

"Well how can I get my father and mother back together again if she starts getting interested in someone else?" She waited through another puzzling few seconds of silence.

"Mallory, I think it's high time you came to terms with things between your parents. Much as you may not like to hear it, your father made the choice to leave the family. It took your mother a long time to recover from it."

Mallory couldn't deny that. Her thoughts shot back to the many times she'd heard her mother crying alone in her room.

"Most people eventually get over their feelings for the person they were once with, and even if the opportunity arose," Aggie continued with a sigh, "they may never want that person back in their life again. That's how it is with your mom. She's moving on."

Mallory couldn't deny that her father's decisions had changed everyone's life.

"Your dad wanted to walk a different path, one that didn't include you and Ron and your mom. I'm sorry if that sounds harsh, but those are the cold hard facts, and unfortunately, how *you* feel about them is not going to change a thing."

The phone went silent again.

"I guess you're right," Mallory finally whispered. She fell back against her pillow, her chest tight with pain.

Aggie's voice softened. "If you love your mother, and I know you do, the most important thing now is to support her. She deserves to be happy, doesn't she?"

"Yes," Mallory whispered again.

"Growing up is never easy, Mallory. It demands a lot from us. We may not always understand the whys and the wherefores or where our paths take us, but we have to believe it's all in divine right order. After all, God never makes a mistake, does he?" Aggie's voice was soothing.

"I guess not," Mallory said, reluctantly. "And Kevin is a nice person. He'd be good for Mom."

"I think so. And if he's not, your mom will figure it out soon enough. She's a very smart lady, you know. After all, look who she got it from!"

"Well, I hope I got some of that smartness, too," Mallory murmured.

"That goes without saying. In fact, I think you got more than all of us."

"More even than Ron?"

"His intelligence is academic, yours is what they call fluidic. And in my book, that's the best kind to have."

Sometimes Aggie sounded incredibly smart.

"One day you'll have to explain that to me, Aggie," Mallory said, "but right now I have to go. I hear Mom calling me to dinner."

Aggie laughed. "Off you go then. Call me Monday when you and Kyle get back from the museum. I'll be on pins and needles until I hear what you've discovered."

Mallory hung up the phone. She jumped off the bed and hurried down the stairs to the dining room unaware that behind her a soft yellow light had begun to spiral up from Ron's stack of Egyptian books. At the same time a hot desert wind swirled in through the half-open window, grabbed at the yellow light and whisked back out again with no one knowing a thing.

The following day, Lorna Gilmartin decided to invite Kevin to dinner at their house instead of going out. Deciding she had to make the best of it, Mallory waited until the last minute before entering the dining room. The aroma of her favorite meal, baked cheese casserole, drifted in from the kitchen taking some of the sting out of her feelings toward Kevin's intrusion.

Involved in an intense conversation with Ron, the Boston architect broke off to greet Mallory warmly as she pulled out a chair and slumped across from him at the table. "Looks like you're reading up on ancient Egypt," he said, turning back to acknowledge Ron's open book.

"No reading material while we're eating!" Lorna called from the kitchen.

"Okay, mom," Ron grinned and closed his book. He looked over at Kevin to explain. "Mallory's class went to Midville a few days ago to see the Egyptian exhibit on display at the museum there. I'm helping her with her school assignment on it."

Kevin nodded in understanding. "A few years ago I was hired to do an architectural job in Egypt," he said. "Spent three months there."

Mallory stared at him, intrigued. "Egypt? Really? Did you

like it?"

"Loved it," Kevin said. "It also gave me a chance to visit the sphinx and the pyramids. I'm really into ancient Egyptian history, you know."

"You saw the sphinx and the pyramids?" she gasped.

"Yes, I went inside the Great Pyramid of Giza," Kevin said, "but with the sphinx, you can only walk around it. There are rumors of a tunnel or passageway under the monument, but so far nobody's found anything."

Lorna carried the last of the platters of food into the dining room and sat down. She beckoned everyone to start fixing a plate.

"So, who do you think built the pyramids," Mallory asked Kevin, her earlier frustration gone.

Kevin spooned himself a serving of casserole. "There are a few schools of thought on that, Mallory. Personally, I believe the Great Pyramid and sphinx are much older than is currently believed."

Ron looked up interested. "Older than 25,000 years?"

"Yes, could be closer to 43,000 years," Kevin stopped to take a bite of his casserole then turned to Lorna in surprise. "Fantastic!" he said, his mouth full. "You should market this. You'd make a fortune."

Clearly embarrassed, Lorna shrugged. "It's my mother's recipe. She taught me how to make it."

"Aggie knows how to cook this?" Mallory stared at her mother stunned. "She never told me that!"

"Yes," Lorna replied. "And she makes it far better than me."

Mallory's eyes narrowed. So Aggie had been holding out on her. She knew how much Mallory loved cheese casserole and yet she'd never said a word about it. Never even offered to make it for her. There's no way to trust that woman, Mallory thought grimly as she resumed eating.

"Getting back to what we were talking about," she heard Ron ask Kevin, "who do *you* think built the pyramids?"

"It's pretty clear the Great Pyramid was built using a very advanced form of technology. Even by today's standards it's considered the most precisely built and accurately aligned building ever constructed in the world." Kevin shook his head as if baffled. "It just doesn't make sense that its only purpose was to be used as a tomb for one person. And as for who built the Great Pyramid . . . ?" he gave a grin before resuming. "Well, maybe an ancient race of aliens."

Aliens? Well, that's a new concept, Mallory thought.

"The exhibit in Midville has a sarcophagus with the mummy of a female singer in it," she told Kevin. "They found it in a tomb in the Valley of the Kings and it has carved wings on the outside that wrap all around the coffin."

"Sounds like this muse probably lived some time during the Middle Kingdom period–perhaps the end of the 14th-17th dynasty," Kevin said. "My understanding is that the purpose of wraparound wings carved on coffins was to protect the deceased."

"Isn't the Middle Kingdom also the period when they started putting ushabtis in tombs?" Lorna said.

"I believe so," Kevin nodded.

Mallory sighed. Even her mother seemed to know something about ancient Egypt. Perhaps it was time to read the books Ron had loaned her.

The discussion about ancient Egypt continued a bit longer with Kevin insisting Mallory and Ron call him in Boston if they had any more questions on Egyptian history. After dinner Lorna suggested they play a game of Scrabble.

Mallory turned to Kevin. "I'm pretty good at this game," she warned.

"Well, I'm pretty good at it myself," he replied, a twinkle in his eyes as he stood to help clear the table.

The day was clear and the sun shining directly overhead as Kyle and Mallory pedaled through the woods the following day on their way to Midville.

"Don't forget," Kyle said, "I have to be home in time for dinner so we've got to get in the museum, snoop around and get out. Pronto."

"Don't sweat it," Mallory assured him. "We're simply there to check it out after hours. It'll be a breeze."

Kyle sighed. "That's what scares me most about you Mallory. You say things first, and then check with your brain later."

"True," Mallory giggled.

"I still think it's a crazy idea to hide in the museum after everyone leaves. We'll get into a lot of trouble if we're caught."

"You worry too much, Kyle." Mallory shrugged.

She rode a bit longer before adding, "Ron loaned me some books on ancient Egypt. I read them until two o'clock this morning. He said he got them from the local library."

"Probably the same books I borrowed a year ago."

"You've read them already! Why didn't you tell me?"

"Well, how could I know Ron would check those books out and you would read them? In case you've forgotten, it's not me who's psychic!" Kyle snapped, and pedaled off in a huff.

Mallory skirted around a pothole and caught up to him. "Okay, you're right, I'm sorry. But here's what I thought was interesting. That ushabti statue that keeps turning around in the museum, well apparently the Egyptians would sometimes leave hundreds of those same statues in a tomb with the dearly departed."

Kyle nodded. "Yeah, they believed the statues would magically come to life in the Underworld, and like servants, do the work for whoever it was that kicked the bucket."

Mallory grinned. "Sounds like those kings and queens weren't about to scrub any floors or do their own laundry, huh?"

Kyle let out a snort of laughter. "My room could use a couple of those statues right now."

"Mine too," Mallory said. "But I wonder why that particular ushabti statue Mrs. Danner told us about keeps moving?"

"Maybe it's trying to tell us it doesn't like this cold Virginia weather."

At this, the wooded area suddenly darkened and grey clouds moved swiftly across the sun, turning the air cold and frigid.

Kyle shivered and stared skyward. "That's weird. Looks like it's going to rain or something."

"Then you shouldn't have said anything about our Virginia weather. With all this strange Egyptian stuff going on, who knows what we're dealing with."

Kyle stopped his bicycle to stare puzzled into the woods. A wind appeared to be whipping fiercely at the trees, yet he could hear no sound.

"I also read in those books," Mallory continued, "that the soul of the dead person had to pass through lakes of fire and pits filled with snakes before they could get to the afterlife."

"Mallory!" Kyle shouted. "Something's wrong here."

Mallory spun her bike around and rode back to where Kyle stared mesmerized.

A silent ferocious wind was whipping through the foliage. Everything about it felt wrong. "Let's get out of here," Mallory shouted as the forest turned even darker. She jumped back on her bike and pedaled at breakneck speed from the area.

Kyle followed, his heart racing.

Behind them the woods returned to normal.

"That was way too spooky," Kyle said for the umpteenth time as they rode into Midville.

"I agree," Mallory said. "It's like someone is trying to scare us away from going into the museum."

Kyle gave an exaggerated shiver. "Maybe we should rethink this, Mallory. It's not too late to back out, you know."

Mallory frowned, but did not answer. Perhaps Kyle was right.

But the time they arrived outside the museum and hid their bicycles in the bushes, Mallory's concern had lessened. Checking the way was clear, she and Kyle slipped out from behind the green hedges and strolled casually up the steps to the Will Call counter.

A woman sat behind the window, her hair as red as her wrap-around Egyptian style tunic. After checking out their names she handed over two passes. Thanking her, Mallory and Kyle hurried inside and joined a group of people waiting in the foyer. Within moments a short, bald-headed man wearing a ridiculously large toga scurried toward them, his floppy brown sandals slapping noisily on the tiled floor.

"Good morning," he said. The man's small mean eyes darted around the group before coming to a rest on Mallory and Kyle. "Shouldn't you two be in school?" he asked, somewhat annoyed.

Mallory took an immediate dislike to the oily-voiced man. "No, we don't have class today," she said. "Our teacher is attending meetings."

With a shrug of indifference the man turned back to the group. "My name is Mortimus Claxley. I'm Assistant Head Curator here. Miss Eleanor Snodgrass will be your docent for the tour today," he said, adjusting his fake headpiece when he saw the docent heading their way.

Eleanor Snodgrass, in the same long white robe and black wig, greeted the tour group with her usual tight smile. When she spotted Mallory and Kyle, she glared suspiciously at them for a moment then glanced furtively at Mortimus Claxley.

"Odd," Mallory muttered to Kyle.

Kyle agreed. He had seen the uneasy look pass between the two badly costumed people, and it did not make him feel good.

Mallory moved closer to the docent. "Wondered if we might join you," she said sweetly, holding up her writing pad. "Need to take a few more notes on the Egyptian exhibit."

Miss Snodgrass frowned and with an impatient sniff, spun on the heels of her very serviceable shoes and headed for the tomb entrance. The group followed eagerly.

Mallory was again hit by stifling hot musty air but followed the camera-carrying visitors past the life-sized statues and display cases until they came to a table with a number of hand-held mirrors made of highly polished copper. On the same table sat a carved chest, small wooden containers, and an assortment of Egyptian bracelets and amulets.

"I don't remember seeing all this stuff before," Mallory whispered to Kyle.

"Just thinking the same thing," Kyle whispered back.

The docent's dull, monotonous voice drifted toward them. "The pharaoh's wife had a vast array of items to make herself look beautiful." She pointed to the small boxes. "She kept her makeup in these containers."

But Mallory wasn't listening. She had moved toward a piece of jewelry displayed on the table. Noticing Mallory's interest, the docent walked over. "This necklace is inlaid with turquoise, lapis lazuli, and red carnelian, precious stones of that time. It was worn like a collar around the neck and across the shoulders."

"Looks pretty heavy to be a necklace," Mallory frowned.

The woman ignored Mallory's remark and continued with her explanation. "In the center is what is called the Wedjat, or *Eye of Horus*. It's an ancient Egyptian symbol. If you look closer, you'll see its center is shaped like a large eye."

The visitors leaned in, *oohing* and *aahing*.

Pleased at this reaction, the docent carried on. "The ancients believed that amulets like this gave the wearer magical protection. They also believed the symbol increased royal power and good health–"

To everyone's surprise, Miss Snodgrass suddenly broke off and staggered back from the table, her eyes blinking rapidly in confusion.

"Are you all right, Miss Snodgrass?" someone asked, but the severe woman simply turned and lurched across the floor, disoriented and bewildered. She came to a stop beside a gigantic urn filled with tall ostrich feathers and gazed around perplexed before moving on. The puzzled group chased after her.

"Kyle, what's wrong with Miss Snotgrass?" Mallory asked.

Kyle was studying a glass case filled with ancient writings, unaware of what had taken place. "You mean Snodgrass?" he asked distracted.

"No, I mean Snotgrass. Did you see what just happened?"

Kyle looked up to see the befuddled woman come to a stop beside a large gilded chariot.

"No, I wasn't watching," he shrugged. He turned back and pointed into the glass case. "Bet you didn't know that records in the time of the Pharaohs were written by scribes on papyrus paper like this."

Mallory rolled her eyes. "Well, if I didn't know before, I certainly do now," she snapped, annoyed that Kyle seemed so disinterested in what was happening.

The tour group stood whispering amongst themselves, confused by the docent's odd behavior. "Are you sure you're all right?" they asked her again.

Eleanor Snodgrass dabbed at the perspiration gathered on her forehead and struggled to regain her composure. "Yes, I'm fine thank you," she nodded, her voice stiff and hollow and her eyes glassy as she meandered off again.

But Eleanor Snodgrass seemed to be having difficulty remembering her script. She glossed over a few obscure facts regarding the gilded chariot, which they were now nowhere near, then turned and led them toward the mummy room. After everyone had squeezed into the small enclosure, she seemed more composed and began to recite the history of the mummified remains of the young temple singer. Having already heard it, Mallory ambled over to the statue of the jackal god, Anubis. He sat immobile on his gilded shrine guarding the ancient mummy. Leaning closer to his wooden face, Mallory whispered, "I dare you to blink now." But Anubis simply stared out solid and unmoving.

"Around the sarcophagus were wreaths of sacred leaves, mimosa, and the blue flowers of the water lilies," Miss Snodgrass rattled on.

"Wow, that muse must have been pretty well liked," someone commented.

"Yes, among other things, she danced and performed at religious ceremonies and became what might be called the pop star of her day," the docent informed them.

Kyle joined Mallory still examining the jackal god. "Did you know that after someone died," he said softly, "their organs were put in special vases and a scarab beetle was placed in the body in place of the heart."

"That's absolutely correct," Miss Snodgrass agreed with a rare smile. "The Egyptians believed that once the deceased reached the afterlife, their heart would be weighed against a feather."

"Weighed against a feather?" a voice exclaimed. "That doesn't make sense."

"Maybe not to us," the docent replied, "but it did to the Egyptians. They believed that if the scale showed the heart was as light as a feather, the soul would be permitted to pass into the Underworld."

"Didn't they also carve magical writings on the scarab to stop the heart from speaking out during the *'heart and feather trial'*?" Kyle said.

"Correct again!" said the pleased docent. She appeared to be back to her old self.

Mallory moved closer, her interest piqued. "So, what did it mean if your heart weighed more than a feather?"

"That your heart was heavy with bad deeds."

"And if that happened," someone in the group added in a spooky voice, "you'd be eaten by Ammut the Devourer God."

"And go straight to hell!" offered another with a blood-curdling, sinister laugh.

Eleanor Snodgrass reared back, horrified at such irreverence.

Mallory stifled a laugh. Perhaps getting into ancient Egypt's version of heaven wasn't quite as appealing as it might at first have seemed. But at that moment Mallory felt the hairs on her neck prickle. She swung around to see the solemn dark-skinned security guard studying her intently from the doorway. Dressed in the same white linen wrap, he now held a steel-tipped spear. Before Mallory could find Kyle, the man had slipped back into the shadows out of sight.

"I don't understand why that guard keeps watching us like that," Mallory said, when Kyle finally joined her. "On top of that, this time he was holding a long spear."

"A spear, huh? Can't say I've seen any other costumed employee walking around holding any props. Not even Miss Snodgrass."

"Good point," Mallory murmured, puzzled.

"And now," the docent addressed the tour group, "you may wander through the exhibit and study it at your leisure. I'll be here on the floor for another half hour if anyone has any questions."

After the room emptied, Mallory hurried over to ask. "Miss Snodgrass, we were wondering where we might find the museum's Egyptian statue that keeps moving?"

The woman staggered back. Her eyes grew wide in alarm and her face paled. "How do you know about that statue?" she gasped.

"Well, I think I heard it from someone in my class," Mallory murmured, baffled at the woman's reaction.

"The s-s-statue has been moved," the docent stammered. "No one may see it."

The light in the room suddenly dimmed and to Mallory and Kyle's horror, the docent appeared to rise up in height. Her long shadow stretched menacingly toward them.

"Beware the Eye of Horus," she snarled at them in a threatening voice.

With rage-filled eyes she glided from the room leaving the bewildered teens staring after her, stunned and shocked.

Chapter 11

"**W**as that ghoulish, or what?" Mallory gasped.

Kyle stared after the disappearing docent. "More disturbing than ghoulish."

"So who is this Horus dude anyway?"

"All I remember about Horus is that the Egyptians believed he was the king of all the ancient gods."

"Well, as long as we watch out for his eye we should be okay," Mallory said, dismissing the threat with a shrug.

But Kyle wasn't so sure. He shuddered involuntarily as they followed each other from the mummy room.

Skirting the exhibit they found their way to the main offices. After drawing a directional map in her notebook, Mallory hunted for the basement. It wasn't far so she drew another map.

"I'd hate to go down there by myself," Kyle whispered as he stared into its dark gloomy depths.

To kill time until the museum closed, Mallory and Kyle took the marble staircase up to the second floor where they kept the guns and uniforms worn by Virginian's Civil War Confederate soldiers, another of Kyle's favorite periods in history.

Before long, after the visitors were alerted the museum would close in ten minutes. Unobserved, Mallory and Kyle slipped quietly into the mummy room.

"This is feeling less and less like a good idea, Mallory," Kyle grumbled, as they ducked behind the sarcophagus.

"True," agreed Mallory, but the excitement dancing in her eyes belied any concern she might have had.

Ten minutes later, crouched uncomfortably behind the sarcophagus, they listened as the last of the visitors and staff exited the building and the front door clanged shut. When the museum fell silent the main lights were switched off, replaced by low security lights that sent gloomy shadows scurrying into all the dark corners.

Fifteen minutes passed and then Mallory decided it was safe to come out. She turned to whisper to Kyle, but he appeared to have fallen asleep. She gave his arm a hard bump.

"Huh?" Kyle opened his eyes to find Mallory studying him impatiently. "Just thinking," he whispered.

He was about to stand up, but dropped down again at the sound of two people in a heated conversation, come to a stop outside the mummy room.

"What do you mean they knew about the moving statue?" one of the voices snapped.

The muffled reply was too low to hear.

The first voice spoke again, this time much more menacingly. "I agree. They're way too nosey." There was a long pause. "We can't afford to have it go down now. Deal with them in whatever way you have to. After all, that's why I hired you."

The two moved away, their conversation fading into the distance.

"Holy smoke, I think they were talking about us," Kyle gasped, his voice shaking.

"Sounded like it," Mallory frowned. "Who do you think they were?"

"That nasty one was Mortimus Claxley. I'd recognize his whiney voice anywhere, but what's with, '*deal with them in whatever way you have to*'?"

"Idle threats," Mallory frowned. "Still, we'd better be on our toes." She glanced over the top of the sarcophagus before turning back at Kyle. "Who do you think the other person was?"

"Miss Snodgrass."

"Snotgrass!" Mallory shook her head. "Are you sure? I couldn't tell if the voice was a man or a woman."

"Trust me, it was the docent. I recognized her clunky heels when she walked away."

"You did? That's very impressive, Watson!" Mallory whispered, pleased at Kyle's sudden powers of deduction.

Kyle continued talking in a low voice. "But now we have another problem."

"Such as?"

"With everyone leaving late and those two holding us up, we've run out of time. We won't be able to hunt for both the statue and check out the basement as well. I have to be home before dark, so it's going to have to be one or the other," Kyle said.

Mallory thought for a moment. "We'll split up then. I'll check Mr. Jarman's office, and you can search the basement."

"Me . . . down there . . . by myself?" Kyle's voice cracked.

"Right. You're not scared are you?" Mallory raised a questioning eyebrow.

"Course I am. I hate going into dark underground places."

"I'll meet you there as soon as I'm done."

Mallory rummaged through her book bag. "And don't turn on any lights," she cautioned, handing him a small flashlight. "We don't want anyone to know we're still here."

Kyle sighed as he took the flashlight and Mallory's crude map of directions. "This is just the kind of crazy thing that keeps getting us into trouble," he muttered to himself before slipping out of the room.

Kyle's knees trembled and his breath escaped in short pants as he zigzagged across the museum floor. Skirting around the column of fierce granite warriors he soon came to the basement and hurried down the stairs.

"There'd better not be any rats in here," he muttered, stepping inside. "I hate rats."

His flashlight lit up a long workbench spread with broken pottery and old bones. Beneath the table were boxes filled with various items of antiquity and numerous packing crates leaned against the wall with *Property of the Egyptian Museum, Cairo* stenciled across them. Beside the crates stood a number of tall shelving units. Kyle moved closer, then staggered back, aghast. The shelves were crammed with human skulls!

At that moment a cold draft swept over him and a deep sigh echoed through the catacomb-like room. Heavy breathing followed.

"Who's there?" Kyle gasped, aiming his flashlight into the darkness.

No one answered.

He called again. "I said, who's there?"

The deep sighing and heavy breathing continued, followed by

a sudden loud clang. Kyle searched for the source of the strange noise and soon discovered a large furnace turning itself on and off as it heated the radiators on the floors above.

Relieved, he continued his search, looking inside old cabinets, under tables, and behind antique furniture stacked hidden from the world. In the warm dry basement air, Kyle suddenly realized he had to sneeze. Burying his face in the crook of his arm he let out a stifled, "tshoo" but now, off balance, staggered backwards, banging his flashlight against a large object beside him. A metallic ring reverberated through the basement. Kyle stood rigid, but to his relief no one came racing down the steps to investigate, so he resumed his search.

However, along with the clanging and whisperings, Kyle had the uncomfortable feeling he was being watched. "Get a grip, dude," he mumbled crossly. "It's those skulls wanting to know what you're up to, that's all."

About to laugh at his own twisted sense of humor, Kyle came to a stunned halt. There stuffed behind a shelving unit was a small oak chest. Mystifying symbols carved across its curved lid glowed back in unusual shades of fluorescent green in the beam of his flashlight. With his discomfort gone, Kyle knelt to lift the lid. Inside he discovered folded blue silk robes, and a thick leather book. Each was marked with the same unusual symbols as on the trunk lid. Kyle grabbed the tome and hurried back to the workbench. Pushing the pieces of pottery and bones to one side he laid the book down and opened it to the first page. After glancing at the text, he realized he could make no sense of the curious language and drawings scrolled inside. Convinced the book was what Mortimus Claxley had been reading the night Mrs. Danner interrupted him, Kyle tucked the heavy manual under his arm and prepared to leave. The ushabti would have to wait.

At that moment he heard a soft rustling noise.

"Mallory, is that you?" he called softly.

There was no answer.

The soft rustling noise sounded again, closer this time.

Kyle's neck went icy cold. He hoped it wasn't rats.

"Mallory?" he repeated, his knees trembling.

Suddenly he was grabbed from behind. A harsh guttural voice breathed a string of curses in his ear and a damp cloth was pressed hard against his nose. The last thing Kyle remembered as chloroform overcame him and his knees buckled was a sharp voice giving the command: "You know what to do. Get rid of him."

Kyle was in trouble.

Mallory waited until Kyle had left the mummy's room and disappeared into the shadows before making her exit. Her great idea about staying in the museum after hours suddenly didn't feel like such a great idea after all. In fact, she was having a hard time shaking the feeling that something was terribly wrong with their plan. Well, hers actually.

Pushing aside her concerns, Mallory hurried through the exhibit halls and down the corridor to the administrative offices. The glass panel on Mr. Jarman's office door was cracked, probably from the recent so-called gas explosion, but she could still make out his name etched on the front. Thankfully the door was unlocked. Making sure no one was in the corridor, she turned the handle and slipped inside.

An oversized mahogany desk graced the center of the room and a bookshelf ran the length of one wall, its shelves groaning with the weight of thick manuals and large three-ring binders. In one corner stood a credenza with a small table lamp glowing softly.

Mallory hurried over to the desk and opened each drawer. Most held hanging folders crammed with papers, but no ushabti. She made her way to a tall glass case. Its shelves held a number of artifacts and between a collection of ivory perfume flasks and leather-covered jars sat a small wooden box, the perfect size for an ushabti. But the door to the glass cabinet was locked.

Mallory hurried over and pulled on the handle of the desk's center drawer hoping to find a key. But the drawer wouldn't budge more than an inch and even though she yanked at it a number of times, it stayed stuck. She was about to give up when she gave it one more violent tug. It jerked open sending pencils, rulers, paperclips and other small items flying into the air.

"Oh, that's just dandy," Mallory grumbled as she knelt down to search through the scattered contents. Disappointed at finding no key, she replaced everything back in the drawer and shoved it closed.

She returned to the locked antiquities case. Short of breaking the glass, there was no way to check out the small box inside. The ticking of a pendulum wall clock reminded her that time was running out, so she turned to leave. As she stepped into the hallway, Mallory suddenly heard footsteps. She pulled the door closed then ducked out of sight behind a large floor-to-ceiling tapestry hanging on the wall.

The echoing strides seemed to go on forever, coming neither closer nor farther away. Finally they stopped, leaving only the intermittent hiss of a nearby radiator. Slipping from her hiding place, Mallory crept across the shadowed floor toward the exhibit. But she had hardly gone any distance when she suddenly found herself confronted by the imposing figure of what looked like the costumed security guard.

The man's eyes glistened intently as he studied her, silent and accusing. Mallory waited, her mouth dry and her heart pounding, but when the strange-acting man made no effort to say anything, she looked closer. With a sigh of relief she realized it was nothing more than a life-size granite sculpture. With her fear growing,

Mallory hurried on to the basement and was soon stepping into the underground crypt.

"Kyle?" she called softly.

No one answered. She called again, this time louder.

Where could he be?

At that moment her foot brushed against something lying on the ground.

Horrified she realized it was Kyle's flashlight. Beside it lay a familiar pair of glasses; the lenses cracked and the frame bent.

Mallory sank to her knees, confused and frightened. Something bad had happened to her friend.

A faint rustling sound floated up from the depths of the dark maze.

Mallory waited for the odd noise to repeat itself.

But Kyle might not even be here any more, she thought in panic. He could have been kidnapped. She'd better try to get help . . . call Aggie.

And then she heard the rustling sound again, this time followed by a muffled moan.

Mallory grabbed the flashlight and glasses and jumped to her feet. "Kyle, if that's you, give me a sign."

She inched her way into the shadowy corridor, the radiator head pipes hissing a noisy warning above her. The faint moan sounded again, followed by a muffled thud.

It appeared to be coming from one of the large crates propped against the wall. Mallory hurried over and tapped softly on the box, but there was no response. She reached to push the lid to one side then stopped, hit by a startling thought. What if it's not Kyle? What if some kind of monstrous animal had accidentally been imported from Egypt and trapped inside the crate, has been waiting to be released?

Mallory pushed aside her out-of-control fears and called again. "Kyle, where are you?"

A second moan drifted out from the box.

Mallory tried to open the crate, but found the lid had been nailed shut.

She hurried back to the workbench to look for something to pry it open. On a shelf beneath the skulls she found a long crowbar. Mallory grabbed it and hastened back to the crate. She pried at the lid until it released with a loud crack. There beneath mounds of packing material she found Kyle, his mouth taped and his hands and feet bound with rope.

"Who did this to you?" Mallory gasped, yanking the tape from his mouth.

The strong odor of chloroform drifted toward her as Kyle shook his head trying to clear his fogged brain. "Didn't see who it was," he stammered weakly. "Someone grabbed me around the neck just after I found a chest with a strange book inside."

Mallory gawked at him in surprise. "A chest? With a book?"

"Right, but I'm sure everything's gone now."

Mallory threw Kyle's bindings aside and handed him his broken glasses.

"Oh, no!" Kyle groaned. "When my parents see these, I'll be on a one way trip to Siberia."

"Let's worry about that later. We need to get out of here, and quick." She dusted off his flashlight and handed it back to him.

But before they could move, they heard the rusty-hinged basement door swing to a close. A moment later a key turned in the corroded lock.

Kyle groaned in despair. "Oh, no, we'll never get out now. We're doomed!"

As if in answer, a sudden wind whipped through the darkened crypt. It thrashed about in a frenzy enclosing them in a thick cloud of dust.

"This is getting really macabre, Mallory," Kyle said, choking on the powdery dirt.

And then, as suddenly as it had begun, the wind stopped and the wall of dust collapsed.

Puzzled, Mallory aimed her flashlight around the basement. "There must be another exit in here somewhere."

But as they peered into the darkness they were overpowered by the pungent smell of musky incense. This was followed by an odd hissing sound. In the beam of their flashlights a huge cobra sat coiled on the floor, its fanged mouth open wide as if ready to strike.

"In case you don't know, I hate snakes, too," Kyle whispered, backing away from the dangerous creature.

"Its eyes are red," Mallory cautioned. "Don't stare into them. It might put you in a trance."

"A trance? Oh, now that's just great. We're going to die down here and no one will ever know it was because a poisonous snake hypnotized us first!"

"C'mon, Kyle. We've been in tighter spots than this."

"We have? When?"

"Can't remember right now," Mallory breathed, backing up beside him. "I'll let you know when I do."

They watched transfixed as the snake swayed from side to side, its eyes glowing bright crimson. But strangely enough, the blue- and green-scaled creature seemed to make no attempt to strike at them. Minutes passed and then Mallory whispered to Kyle.

"You know, there's something peculiar about that snake."

"Yeah, it can't seem to make up its mind which one of us to kill first."

"I'm going to throw something at it to see if I'm right."

"Are you crazy? One move and that snake will get us in seconds."

Mallory let fly her torch at the swaying reptile. To Kyle's astonishment, the flashlight passed straight through it.

"Holy smoke!" he gasped. "It's some kind of apparition."

"Exactly. I could see the faint outline of the wall behind it. Didn't mean to scare you, but that's the only way I could test out my theory."

"Theory?"

"Yeah, I had a feeling about it so I went with that."

"You went with nothing more than a feeling?" Kyle exclaimed, as the apparition began to fade.

"I thought there might be some kind of magic spell involved," Mallory grinned. "And I was right."

"But what if you'd been wrong?" Kyle was breathing hard.

"Well, I wasn't. And now that you're less woozy, let's see if we can find another way out of here–"

Mallory stopped abruptly at the sound of a key turning in the rusty basement lock. They turned to watch as the door swung slowly open. Kyle yelled, grabbed both their book bags, and bolted for the stairs, but Mallory hung back wondering if it might be another trap. Deciding otherwise, she raced after him.

They sprinted up the spiral staircase back to the museum unaware that the shadow of their rescuer was racing out of sight just a few steps ahead of them.

Once they were back on the first floor, Mallory and Kyle sprinted for the front doors. Behind them the museum suddenly lit up in a brilliant flash of light, followed by the sound of running feet.

"I command you to stop!" an angry voice bellowed.

But the two teenagers had no intention of stopping. They raced across the foyer and through the unlocked doors, taking the steps two at a time. As they reached the bottom, a backfiring van covered in giant-sized museum posters careened up the street and skidded to a stop beside them.

"Jump in, I've got your bikes!" shouted a familiar voice through the open window.

Mallory hesitated for a moment, stunned at her grandmother's appearance. Aggie motioned frantically toward the van's open side door. In seconds the two escaping intruders leapt into the back seat and slid the door shut behind them. Aggie spun her steering wheel to the left and with her foot hard to the accelerator, peeled away just as Mortimus Claxley appeared through the front doors. He watched frustrated as the VW screeched around the corner and disappeared from view.

Inside the van no one spoke as Aggie gunned the engine to its limit. It was not until she urged the vehicle onto the main highway leading back to Cedar Creek that she gave a sigh of relief, eased her foot off the pedal, and relaxed back in her seat.

"Thanks, Aggie." Mallory panted, still breathless from their narrow escape. "Guess we needed you after all."

"You sure did, girl. I waited out of sight for a while, but when it got late and there was no sign of either of you, I suspected you might be in trouble. I discovered your bikes, loaded them on board and hung back until I saw the front doors come crashing open." She glanced into her rear view mirror at the two escapees. "Figured it might be you two. That's when I took off."

Aggie removed her dark glasses and turned down the collar of the over-sized trench coat she was wearing.

"Well, I guess your disguise answers the question of why you're wearing that poodle," Kyle said.

"Poodle?"

"Yeah. The one sitting on your head."

Aggie let out a loud guffaw and pulled the curly blonde wig from her head. "I've got a whole wardrobe like this. You never know when it might come in handy."

"Yeah, especially if you're hanging around with Mallory," Kyle said, wiping his brow.

Mallory giggled. "Why did you put all those posters on your van, Aggie?"

"Well, I decided you were right and it was too identifiable with all its painted psychedelic peace signs," Aggie explained, "I wasn't sure at first what I was going to do. Thought I'd wait until I got to Midville, but when I saw stacks of posters being thrown away in the museum's garbage cans, I grabbed them. They already had tape stuck all over them which it made it real easy to attach them to my trusty old van."

Mallory shook her head and smiled. "Honestly Aggie, you've missed your calling."

"Calling or not, I'm really glad you were there," Kyle said, still shaken from his escape.

Aggie glanced over her shoulder. "Where are your glasses, young man?"

Kyle removed the damaged glasses from his pocket and reached over the seat to show her. "My dad's gonna strangle me when he sees these."

"Oh, boy," Aggie said, with a shake of her head. "So things did get serious. You better tell me what happened."

Mallory took a deep breath. "Well, we carried out our plan and hid in the mummy room. After the museum closed Kyle went to search the basement and I left to look through Mr. Jarman's office for the ushabti statue. I couldn't find it though. I think he must have locked it away in one of his cabinets."

"And down in the basement I found a wooden chest with a strange book inside," Kyle added. "There were also some robes with symbols embroidered all down the front."

Mallory turned to Kyle in surprise. "You didn't tell me about any robes!"

"That's because I was too busy trying not to get killed!"

Aggie rammed on the brakes and skidded over to the side of the highway. "Good Lord!" she said, turning to face them. "Did things get that bad?"

Kyle told her about someone shoving a rag soaked with chloroform in his face and then locking him in a crate.

"Bad guys, obviously," Mallory shrugged.

"Obviously!" Aggie's voice had raised a full octave. "And locking you in a crate?!"

"It's all right, Aggie," Kyle said. "Mallory found me and set me free."

"Or you wouldn't be here," Aggie consoled herself. "Still, I'd like to get my hands on whoever did this to you."

"After I found Kyle," Mallory continued, "someone locked the basement door before we could get out. A moment later a snake appeared in front of us."

Aggie's eyes grew wide. "I hate snakes," she said, shivering involuntarily.

"Me too, but it wasn't real, Aggie," Kyle said. "It must have been projected from somewhere. We just didn't stay around long enough to find out from where."

"Good thinking," Aggie nodded. "But how *did* you get out of the basement?"

"Someone unlocked the door and we made a run for it," Mallory said.

"Unlocked the door? Who did?" Aggie asked.

"Don't have a clue," Mallory shrugged. "We never saw our rescuer."

"Hmm, evidently someone wanting to help," Aggie murmured. She started the van again and steered it back onto the highway.

By the time Aggie pulled up outside Kyle's house, the sun had been down more than an hour. She turned off her vehicle and scrambled out.

"Help me get rid of these posters," she whispered, grabbing an armful and stuffing them inside her van.

Within minutes the posters had all been removed and except for the smoking engine, no one would ever have known that Aggie's trusty VW had been used as a get-away car in an incredibly clandestine adventure.

"Now leave your father to me," Aggie said confidently, as Kyle pulled his bike from the back of the van and started wheeling it up the path.

He propped it against the porch, and after opening the front door, led the way inside. "Dad? Mom?" he called nervously.

At the sound of Kyle's voice, Harry Johnson, a tall man with dark bushy eyebrows and a matching moustache, rushed from the kitchen; Kyle's mother close at his heels. She frowned at the bedraggled group shuffling up the hallway toward them.

"Should have known you'd be involved with my son's lateness, Aggie," Kyle's father growled.

"Now, Harry," said Kyle's mother touching his arm. "Let Aggie explain."

"Right," Aggie grinned. "Anyway, you always know Kyle's safe whenever he's with me. Plus it couldn't be helped. We got involved in a project and didn't realize how late it was."

Kyle's father frowned. "Is that the truth, Aggie?"

"Really, Harry," Aggie said, trying to sound offended. "When have you ever caught me in a lie?"

"About once a week for the past twenty years."

Aggie shrugged casually. "Well, there may have been a few times where I stretched things slightly–"

Harry Johnson sighed. He had never won an argument with Aggie where his son was concerned, and he'd learned it was hopeless to even try. However, as he turned to Kyle he suddenly noticed the damaged glasses.

"Not again," he groaned. He shook his head and held his hand up to stop Kyle from explaining. "No, don't even try to tell me what happened," he said. "I can see they're broken."

"Now that's what I like about you, Harry," Aggie grunted. "You always have a frightening grasp of the obvious."

"Well, you know the routine," Kyle's father continued to Kyle. "You'll have to work in the shop until you've paid for a new pair." He sounded firm and unrelenting.

Kyle's parents owned *The Hot Cuppa* coffee shop on Main Street and Kyle often earned money by helping out there after school or on weekends. Now he'd have to work for weeks with no pay.

Kyle sighed, and turned to Aggie. "Thanks for the ride home."

Relieved she would not have to answer any more questions, Aggie grabbed Mallory's arm and steered her toward the door.

Kyle hurried ahead to let them out.

"I'll see you at school tomorrow, Mallory," he mumbled.

"Not unless you're on your way to Siberia," she whispered back.

Kyle looked back puzzled.

"Well, you did mention your father would probably send you there once he saw your broken glasses." With a mischievous grin Mallory sailed out the door after Aggie.

After Aggie dropped her off at home, Mallory was disappointed to learn that Ron had not felt well and decided to go to bed right after dinner. She wanted to tell him about their adventure at the Midville Museum, but instead slipped a note under his door that she'd bring him up-to-date the following day.

Sleep did not come easy for Mallory that night as the strange incident in the basement returned to haunt her. Sometime in the early hours of the morning she awoke startled. Something wasn't right. She felt icy cold. Across the room a bright red glow moved slowly along the wall toward her.

Is there a fire in the house? Panicked, Mallory struggled to get out of bed, but found she couldn't move. Her legs had turned to lead. She watched in horror as the red glow on the wall grew until it filled the whole room. She was about to call for help when she heard the sound of a thin raspy voice.

I am a messenger.

Squeezing her eyes shut and finally able to move, Mallory stumbled up over the pillows. I'm having a nightmare, she thought, cringing back against the headboard.

The voice continued. *You sleep not.*

Mallory's eyes flew open. There on the coverlet sat a large

scarab beetle, its head a glowing pulsating stone of blood red. Was this creature speaking telepathically?

"Who are you, and h-h-how did you get in my room?" Mallory stammered.

The beetle scooted closer.

I entered your bag before you left the museum.

Mallory pressed farther back, clutching the covers under her chin. "What? Where?"

In the room where the muse lies.

Convinced she was still dreaming, she asked, "Why are you here? What do you want?"

Your help.

"Help?"

Hush, she comes.

Mallory looked around, confused. "Who comes?"

The scarab scuttled to the end of the bed and scurried over the edge. Suddenly the room grew unbearably hot and humid. Mallory unclenched the sheet and watched stunned as a white mist began to form on the glassy surface of her standing oval mirror. Curious, she slipped from the bed and crept forward. Within seconds the white mist had melted away and in its place a flowing river bordered by tall date palms began to appear. Along the banks of the wide river were brilliant green farmlands and a village of square-shaped houses. Smoke from cooking fires curled lazily into the air.

Mallory watched mesmerized as an ancient Egyptian barge sailed into view, moving rapidly along the sun-glinting waterway. Beneath an ornamental canopy reclined a young woman flanked by four male attendants. As the vessel pulled closer to shore, a large bird tethered on the flower-strewn deck suddenly screeched out in surprise. Mallory jumped as the sound echoed through her room.

The young woman on the boat, her cobalt black hair falling to her shoulders in a multitude of small braids, stood up surprised then moved quickly to the front of the boat. The river breeze whipped at the long pleated gauzy robe she wore, and sunlight glinted from a headband of turquoise and sparkling stones.

"You can see me?" the girl gasped, staring directly at Mallory.

Chapter 17

Mallory gaped back in disbelief. "Yes, I can see you," she finally answered. "Who are you?"

"I am Nathifa," the girl replied. "By what name are you called?"

"Mallory," Mallory said, dumbfounded at the image in her mirror.

"I am honored to know you, Mal-lor-ree," Nathifa said. A beaded belt hanging low on her hips rattled gently as she turned to beckon to a young girl standing behind her. "This is my handmaiden, Halima."

The Nubian slave stepped forward and gave a slight bow. She was dressed in a linen shift of gossamer fabric and had long silver filigree earrings that brushed gently against her ebony skin. Both young women wore solid gold bands on their upper arms.

At that moment Mallory heard the faint sound of drumbeats and smelled the fragrance of perfumed vegetation wafting into the room. She looked around confused. Could the scent be coming from the image in her mirror?

"I am a muse, a temple singer," Nathifa said.

Mallory recognized the word 'muse' and asked, "Are you the mummy at the Midville Museum?"

"I know not of that," Nathifa frowned. "All I know is that I am trapped here in a World between Worlds."

"I don't understand," Mallory said.

Nathifa sighed before explaining. "You see I once loved a Prince, and he loved me–" She broke off and lowered her head as though in sudden pain.

Halima looked out with a sad smile. "My mistress was poisoned by those in the Egyptian court who did not approve of her association with the ruling Prince," she explained. "I was poisoned at the same time."

Mallory blinked rapidly, not entirely convinced she wasn't still dreaming. "Well, if that's you in the sarcophagus," she informed Nathifa, "you might like to know you were found buried in a royal crypt. You've been there for thousands of years, but no one knows much about you, or why you were put there in the first place."

Nathifa nodded slowly as if she understood. "In the moments before I died," she went on, "the Prince I loved promised we would meet again in the Underworld, but for some reason I cannot find him. I just keep sailing back and forth along this river."

Halima reached for her mistress's hand. "Yes, something prevents us from leaving this strange place," she sighed.

As unbelievable as Nathifa's story sounded, Mallory felt sorrow for the beautiful girl and her loyal handmaiden. "The scarab beetle, does it belong to you?" she asked.

"Yes, the beetle was assigned to protect me until I reached the world beyond."

"Which you can't get to because you're trapped," Mallory finished.

Nathifa nodded.

Mallory leaned closer. "Did you have anything to do with all that shaking at the museum the other day?"

"Yes. I sensed someone could feel our presence and I tried to stop you from leaving. I'm sorry if it caused concern. I am desperate to break the spell trapping us."

"Did you also cause the woods to go dark and cold when my friend and I were on our way to the museum the other day?" Mallory asked.

Nathifa frowned. "No, I do not have the power to change your woods," she said. "I think someone is trying to stop you from helping me."

"Someone like who?"

"Perhaps a priest with powers," Nathifa sighed.

Before she could say more the image in the mirror suddenly turned watery and wavy. "I cannot stay!" she called as the picture began to fade.

"Wait! The beetle said you needed help." Mallory cried. "What kind of help?"

"Find whatever it is that binds me to this place," the muse pleaded, her voice echoing as if from afar. "It is close."

Mallory grabbed the sides of the mirror hoping it might stop the image from disappearing, but in seconds the surface of the glass had returned to normal. She waited to see if Nathifa might appear again, but when nothing happened she went back to bed and soon fell into a deep sleep.

When Mallory awoke next morning and untangled her legs from the twisted sheets, the memory of the whole strange experience with Nathifa came rushing back. Had it all been a dream? She jumped out of bed and hurried to inspect the mirror. Partly lit by the early morning sun, it appeared perfectly normal. Undaunted, Mallory reached for the phone.

"Aggie, I think something strange happened to me last night," she said after her grandmother picked up the receiver.

"Wouldn't surprise me one bit. Want to tell me what it was?"

"Well, I was having trouble sleeping," Mallory began, "or maybe I did fall asleep and then woke up, but–" She broke off, noticing the time on her clock. "Oh, no! Aggie I can't explain now. I've overslept and I'm running late for school. I've got to leave but trust me, it's unbelievable."

"You can't even give me a clue?"

"It has to do with the Egyptian exhibit."

"Probably could have figured that one out for myself." Aggie sounded quite vexed. "All right, teashop . . . after school . . . four o'clock . . . everyone."

Mallory whispered to Ron before he left for school that Aggie wanted to see everyone in the teashop at four o'clock. He confirmed he could make it and would let Victoria know about the meeting when he saw her later in their Home Room.

"Can't be there," Kyle sighed when Mallory told him about it at school. "I have to work for Dad."

"Yeah, about that," Mallory said, as she followed him into the classroom and slid into the desk behind him. "I thought I could help you earn the money you need for new glasses by working at the shop, too. After all, it was kinda my fault you got into all that trouble in the first place."

"Cool, I'll ask Dad. Meantime, what's this meeting about?"

Before Mallory could answer, Mrs. Romano bustled into the room wearing one of her favorite paisley print dresses and a long woolly sweater. "Good morning class," she called out in a cheery voice.

Mallory leaned closer to Kyle, her voice low. "Something weird happened to me last night. I'll call and bring you up to date on everything after you get home from work tonight."

Kyle nodded that he understood.

At four o'clock sharp, Ron and Victoria strode into *Ye Olde Tea Shoppe,* each carrying a stack of books on ancient Egypt. Seeing Mallory sitting at a large round table in the teashop's only sunlit corner, they headed across the floor to join her.

A moment later Aggie said goodbye to her final customer and dashed over. "This is everyone, huh?" she asked, looking around.

Mallory was about to tell them Kyle had to work, when the front door flew open and he strode in, clutching an even bigger stack of books.

"Dad let me off for the day," he grinned, dumping everything onto the table and pulling out a chair. He turned to Mallory. "My father says thanks for the offer, but I have to serve my sentence alone."

"Sentence?" Ron shot Mallory a puzzled look.

"Kyle broke his glasses at the museum yesterday so I offered to work at the coffee shop to help pay for them."

Aggie gestured at Mallory. "Go ahead and tell Ron and Victoria about what actually happened there at Midville while I fix us some drinks and snacks. And everybody cross your fingers I don't have any more customers for a while."

As Aggie bustled off to get refreshments, Mallory and Kyle began by telling them about Miss Snodgrass's odd behavior with the tour group, and the jeweled collar with the Wedjat symbol.

"Later, when Kyle and I asked Miss Snodgrass about the moving statue, she said she didn't know where it was, then told us in a real scary voice to 'Beware the eye of Horus'."

"And you should've seen her change when she said it." Kyle rolled his eyes and gave an exaggerated shiver.

"Horus, hmm," Ron mumbled, and reached to open one of his books. "They call Horus the falcon god," he said, "but I remember reading something else that . . . yes, here it is. It's a warning from the Egyptian Book of the Dead, Spell 177."

"The Egyptians wrote a book for the dead?" Mallory asked, amazed.

Kyle reached for one of the freshly baked pastries Aggie had just set down on the table. "Yeah, it's an ancient tome filled with spells, prayers and maps so dead people can find their way safely to the afterlife," he explained.

"So, what does this spell say?" Aggie asked.

Ron read from the page. ". . . *the red-eyed Horus, violent of power, waits for you . . .*"

"Fantastic!" Kyle mumbled through his pastry. "On top of everything else, now we have an angry god after us."

"You're right about 'angry'," Ron said. "That's what the 'red eye' symbolizes. But this spell was intended for the deceased on their journey to the Underworld, not for people still alive so I think you're probably safe," he laughed.

Aggie patted Kyle on the shoulder. "Now tell Ron and Victoria what else went on at Midville yesterday, and then Mallory can enlighten us about what she went through in her room last night. I don't think I can wait another minute to hear about it."

"Right, well after the museum closed," Kyle began, "I snuck down into the basement to see if I could find anything that would explain Claxley's behavior the night Mrs. Danner caught him down there."

"And I went to search through Mr. Jarman's office, but found nothing," Mallory interjected. She nodded at Kyle to continue his story.

"Well, in the basement I got lucky and found a chest with a curious manuscript and robes inside, but before—" Kyle broke off, swallowing hard as he remembered his attacker.

"It's okay, Kyle," Mallory interrupted. "I'll tell them what happened next."

She explained about Kyle being attacked, finding his broken glasses, and how she freed him from the crate. She also told them about the apparition of the coiled cobra and throwing her flashlight at it.

"A cobra!" Ron cried, almost choking on his muffin. "You took a chance there, Mallory. What if the snake had been real?"

"That's exactly what I told her," Kyle grunted.

"Well, it didn't turn out to be real," Mallory shrugged, "but that overpowering smell of incense was. Any idea what that was all about?"

"I think I can help," Victoria cried excitedly. "I just read something about incense." She grabbed one of her books and ran her finger down the list of contents. "Here," she said, turning to the right page. *"In the time of the pharaohs, incense was referred to as the fragrance of the gods. The gods not only revealed themselves by sight and sound, but also by smell."*

"You mean we had a visit from a god?" Mallory asked, stunned.

"Probably that red-eyed Horus dude," Kyle mumbled.

Ron gave a half grin. "Egypt had so many gods it's hard to know if it would have been a good one, or an evil one."

"Hmm," Mallory said. "And the snake, what does that mean?"

"From what I recall," Ron continued, "serpents were considered a symbol of wisdom. If it was plumed or hooded the way you guys saw it, it usually meant that the wisdom had been given wings."

"I don't get it," Mallory said.

"Well, it could be that someone from beyond was sending a warning to be wise about what you're getting involved in," Aggie suggested.

Victoria grinned. "Kind of like an ancient Egyptian message sent via snake mail."

Following her words the front door suddenly flew open with an ominous bang and in stepped a familiar uniformed figure. Spying everyone in the corner the burly man strode toward them, the tread of his boots heavy and determined.

"Oh, oh," Aggie said under her breath. "I've got a feeling this may not be good."

She smiled up as Cedar Creek's Chief of Police came to a stop towering over them.

"**H**owdy, Aggie, everyone," John Banks said. "I wasn't expecting you all to be here, but it's probably a good thing you are."

"And why is that?" Aggie asked, the picture of innocence.

"A short while ago I had a call from the Midville Police," Banks began. "Seems the museum had a break-in late yesterday and two teenage kids were seen fleeing from the property."

"Kids from Midville, you mean?" Aggie suggested.

"Well, no, that's the thing. The PD in Midville thinks these kids might be from Cedar Creek."

"Why would they think that, Chief Banks?" Ron asked, his face every bit as innocent as Aggie's.

"Seems the museum guard thought he recognized the kids as part of the Cedar Creek school group that had been there a few days earlier."

"Well, guards have made mistakes before," Aggie shrugged.

"True," said the officer, sizing up the older woman. "But then a van was seen picking up these two kids; a noisy VW van covered in museum posters, was the way they put it." He took a deep breath and stared at Aggie before continuing. "You wouldn't know anything about that now, would you, Aggie?"

"Midville Museum? Really, John! Why in the world would I

be in Midville?" Aggie exclaimed. "And for that matter, take a look at my van if you need to. I didn't notice any posters on it when I drove in this morning."

Chief Banks sighed. Aggie was as cunning as a fox and, as usual, a force to be reckoned with.

"I'm not accusing anyone, Aggie," he said, his eyes sweeping over Mallory and Kyle, "but I'd sure appreciate it if the guilty parties, *whoever* they may be, not go back to the museum anytime soon."

"Hopefully they won't," Aggie said. "But what happened at the museum that the Midville police had to go out of their way to call you?"

"They said some valuable glass objects had been broken–"

"Broken?!" Mallory almost choked on the word. Catching herself in time, she changed her tone. "Why, that's horrible. I mean, objects in museums are so . . . valuable."

"Yes, they are," the chief continued. "The Museum didn't give the Midville police any details so it's obvious they're not pressing charges. They just wanted me to give the culprits–*whoever* they may be–a warning."

Reassured that Mallory had calmed down, Aggie focused her steely grey eyes on Banks. "And what makes you think *we* would know anything about this travesty, John?"

"Look, Aggie, don't get huffy," Chief Banks said. "If a complaint is made, I'm obliged to check up on it." He turned to Mallory. "I know you're in the detective business now, Mallory, and I know what a good job you did recently in finding Edna May's missing Ming vase, but if you're in any way involved with whatever is going on at Midville Museum and something goes wrong, I won't be able to protect you–"

He broke off to stare down at the table. "Why all the books

on ancient Egypt?" he asked curiously.

"I'm writing a play about that period for my school drama class," Kyle jumped in. "Everyone's helping me with it."

"A play? On ancient Egypt?" John Banks asked.

"Yeah," Kyle said, calmly holding the officer's astonished stare. "It's called, *The Mummy with the Moldy Breath.*"

Aggie pressed her lips together trying not to laugh as Ron and Victoria squirmed slightly beside her.

Chief Banks turned back to Mallory. "I'm here if you need help," he sighed, "but keep in mind that I do have to uphold the law."

Mallory nodded her thanks as Aggie took over. "Of course you do, Chief, and we appreciate that. Thanks for stopping by."

Thus dismissed, the Police Chief left the teashop shaking his head and hiding his grin. *"The Mummy with the Moldy Breath?"* he mumbled. "Whatever will that lot think of next?"

"Wow, that was awkward," Kyle said, watching through the front window as the constable drove away.

Aggie's brow had furrowed in concern. "Sounds like Claxley's declared war."

Before anyone could reply, the door tinkled again and in bustled the town's elderly librarian, Edna May Florentine, a bundle of books tucked firmly in one arm.

The petite woman scurried toward them, her eyes twinkling and her smile wide. "It's so good to see everybody together again," she said, beaming around the table. "Now, I don't want to interrupt you, but after Kyle left the library earlier today–he stopped by to ask for a particular book on ancient Egypt and told me you were all meeting here–I suddenly remembered I had some very old editions on the subject stored safely away in the back room. Thought I'd bring them by in person."

Miss Florentine placed the books on the table and then stood back expectantly as if waiting for an invitation to join them.

"Nice to see you, Edna May," Aggie finally said, confused as to how to handle this unexpected turn of events.

"Ancient Egypt is one of my favorite subjects," Miss Florentine gushed. "I even took classes in hieroglyphics when I was in college."

Mallory perked up at this. "May I ask you a question then, Miss Florentine?"

The librarian turned with a smile. "Of course you may, dear."

"Well, I saw a piece of jewelry on display at the Midville Egyptian exhibit a few days ago," Mallory began, "and I was wondering if there was a reason why the Egyptians used scarab beetles so much in their jewelry and decorations."

"Oh, yes, indeed, there was a reason," Miss Florentine said, delighted at an opportunity to share. "The scarab beetle was nearly always used as a symbol to show the change of state from death to rebirth." She gestured to the books lying open on the table. "As you may have already noticed in the pictures, many scarab pieces were set with red carnelian stone to represent the beetle's head. The Egyptians often used turquoise and lapis lazuli with the carnelian because they believed that these three stones together would give an item divine powers." She leaned forward, her voice dropping low. "The ancients believed in magic, you know," she added gravely.

"Yes, we've been reading up on all that, Edna May," Aggie muttered.

Fully wound up, the elderly librarian carried on undaunted. "The carnelian stone also represented the rising sun. The Egyptians believed that when the sun set each night it went into the Underworld then rose again the next day to the world of the living. But because the ancient Egyptians also lived in fear the sun might not return from the Underworld, they gave great reverence to the sun god, Amun-Ra, in the hopes he would always look favorably upon them."

Mallory quickly scrawled something in her notebook. "Thank you, Miss Florentine," she said with a smile. "That was very helpful."

"And thank you for stopping by, Edna May," Aggie said, jumping to her feet. She took the woman's arm and gently ushered her toward the front door.

But Edna May was not about to be swayed from her favorite subject that easily. "Of course, you must be careful if you're dabbling in Egyptian mystical rites," she called over her shoulder. "Once certain doors are opened, they cannot be closed, you know."

"We'll watch what we're doing," Aggie said, holding the front door open and guiding the excited woman through. "And if we have any more questions on Egypt we'll be back in touch with you."

Miss Florentine waved goodbye and stepped from the tearoom. But a moment later she popped her head back in. "One more thing. You might like to know the Egyptians believed that when the sun went into the Underworld it resurrected itself at dawn back into the world of the living. That's why they built their tombs to be resurrection machines."

The door slammed shut behind her.

Aggie hurried back to the table. "What is that woman babbling about? Those musty old tombs don't look anything like machines to me, and where were those dead bodies planning on resurrecting to anyway?"

"They believed the tombs were portals that would take them to the afterlife," Kyle said. "When the sun died each night, meaning when it set, it went into the Underworld, made it through, and then resurrected itself again the next morning."

"I wonder how they arrived at that one," Aggie grunted before sitting down. "Glad we don't think that way today. I'd be scared to go to bed at night." She turned to address Mallory. "I have a feeling your question to Edna May about scarab beetles has something to do with what happened last night, granddaughter, so start talking, we're all ears."

At that moment the bell over the door tinkled yet a third time.

"You've got to be kidding!" Aggie said, twisting around impatiently to see who had dared enter her teashop this time.

In the doorway stood Joyce Danner. Spotting everyone in the corner, she made a beeline in their direction.

"Nice to see you again, Joyce," Aggie sighed. "Is there something I can help you with?"

"Sorry to burst in on you like this," Joyce said. "It's just that I overheard Mallory at school telling Kyle you'd all be meeting here today so I thought I'd come by and let you know what my mother just found out." She stopped abruptly when she saw all the open books on the table.

"Oh, don't worry about those," Ron gestured. "We're helping Mallory and Kyle with their class assignment on the Egyptian exhibit."

"I have to finish that assignment, too," Joyce frowned absently.

"And what was it your mother found out, dear?" Aggie gently prodded.

Joyce looked blank for a moment as if she'd forgotten why she was even there. "Oh yes, well, my mother learned from some of the other people working at the museum that Mortimus Claxley has been desperately searching for where Mr. Jarman hid the ushabti statue. She thinks his behavior is kind of suspicious."

"We had the same thought," Mallory said. "Does your mother have any idea where Mr. Jarman may have hidden this statue?"

"She's pretty sure it's in the basement." Joyce stopped for a moment deep in thought then looked over at Mallory. "Maybe that's a good place to start hunting for it."

"Good suggestion," Kyle said, not daring to tell her they had already searched there.

"Well, I can't stay," Joyce said quickly. "Have to pick up some items for Mom." She spun on her heel and headed for the door. With all eyes on her exit, Joyce suddenly turned to say, "Oh, and one other thing. My mother said you might like to know that Mr. Claxley is a trained arcane priest." With no further explanation, she disappeared out the door.

The teashop fell silent.

"Anyone know what an arcane priest is?" Mallory finally asked.

"Nope," Ron grunted and reached for his dictionary. He paged through the book then began to read. "The word arcane means, something understood by few. A person trained in these practices is often called a Wizard of Magic. This obscure esoteric knowledge is considered dark, mysterious, and highly secret."

Aggie nodded thoughtfully. "In light of this little bit of news, I'm inclined to think the snake you saw in the basement might have been a spell Claxley conjured up to scare people away."

"Wow, if Mortimus Claxley has powers like that, then he's one dangerous dude," Kyle exclaimed.

"And when Mrs. Danner ran into him that night, he was probably in the middle of one of his dark arcane rituals," Mallory reminded everyone.

"But why even run the risk of being discovered down there?" Victoria asked. "Why not do it privately in his own home?"

"Perhaps he feels safer doing his magic stuff after hours in the basement when no one's around," Aggie suggested.

Mallory shook her head. "No, something tells me there's another reason why he was in the basement that night conjuring up secret magic, and I'll bet it has something to do with that ushabti."

"Even more reason why we need to find the statue before he does," Aggie said firmly. She paused for a moment before adding, "That's why I intend to go to Midville. I can wear one of my disguises and after the museum closes, I'll search the basement myself."

Mallory shot up in her chair. "Not without me you won't!"

Victoria gasped at her friend. "But you'll be recognized!"

"Not if I wear one of Aggie's disguises."

Aggie grinned, obviously pleased.

Kyle groaned. "I'm not so sure this is a good idea," he said, squirming uncomfortably in his seat.

"Don't worry, Kyle. You don't have to go with us," Mallory said. "Even in disguise, Claxley or Miss Snodgrass might recognize us as the two kids they chased away yesterday. It'd be better if I go alone with Aggie."

"Okay, but what about Aggie's VW?" Kyle said. "You can't cover it with posters again."

"Hadn't thought about that," Aggie frowned. She glanced over at Mallory. "Maybe I can borrow your mom's car. I'll come up with a plausible reason why I need it."

Mallory grinned. She had no doubt Aggie would find a good excuse for needing her mother's car.

Aggie turned to Mallory. "Now tell us what happened to you before anyone else comes through that darn door."

Mallory took a deep breath and pulled her chair up closer.

"So, here's what went on," she said, her voice dropping low. "It was late by the time I fell asleep last night because I kept thinking about everything that had happened to Kyle and me. But I woke a short while later and when I looked across the room I saw something moving along the wall; a blood red glow that kept getting bigger and bigger until the whole room lit up."

"Good Lord," Aggie gasped.

"Then I heard a voice." Mallory continued, which made Aggie gasp even louder.

Mallory went on to tell them about the scarab beetle speaking to her, the image of ancient Egypt appearing in her mirror, and Nathifa's plea for help.

Everyone sat in stunned silence until Mallory had finished her tale.

"So that's why you asked Edna May about the scarab," Victoria finally asked.

"Yes, because Nathifa told me the beetle was assigned to protect her until she reached the world beyond."

"Which she can't get to because something is keeping her trapped in this strange *World between Worlds*," murmured Ron.

Kyle, quiet throughout all of this, spoke up. "Mallory, we had a pretty scary experience at the museum yesterday. Are you sure this wasn't just a dream that felt real?"

"No, Kyle," Mallory said emphatically. "And here's how I know it really happened."

She reached into her backpack and pulled out a small drawstring purse. "This was in front of the mirror when I woke up this morning," she said, loosening the strings and turning the pouch upside down.

To everyone's astonishment, a stream of yellow sand poured from the purse, glinting in the light as it spread out across the table.

"**W**ell, I think it's pretty clear something unusual happened in Mallory's bedroom last night," Aggie said, taking a pinch of the sparkling sand and rubbing it between her fingers. "And I don't have a problem believing it was probably a visitor from ancient Egypt."

Ron nodded. "I agree, and if this Nathifa is not able to get to the afterlife because of something linked to the Midville Museum, then I'd say we definitely need to solve the mystery before the exhibit goes back to Cairo."

Aggie turned to Mallory. "Read us the important clues you've written so far, Mallory. I think we need to go over them."

Mallory opened her notepad and bent her head to read. "Okay, point one: all this weird stuff going on in Midville Museum didn't start until after the arrival of the Egyptian exhibit."

"Which confirms that something in the museum, linked to the mummy, is triggering all this," Kyle said.

Mallory continued. "Point two, an earthquake that's not an earthquake shook the lower floor of the Midville Museum, but Nathifa said she caused that to happen so we have an answer to that point."

"Point three," Mallory continued, "the statue of the jackal

dog, Anubis, blinked at me."

"And to our knowledge, hasn't moved its eyes since," Kyle added.

"Well, I'm not done checking out that wooden-faced god yet," Mallory said. "I just know he's involved in all this."

"Point four, Eleanor Snodgrass is a very suspicious character with multiple personalities."

"How'd you arrive at that one?" Victoria asked, puzzled.

"Like on our field trip when she turned all weird and staggered across the museum floor," Mallory said. "And when she threatened us in a deep voice about that dude, Horus."

"Don't forget to add Mortimus Claxley to your list of suspicious characters," Kyle said.

"I was about to mention that," Mallory said. "Point five, Mrs. Danner comes across Mortimus Claxley doing some strange kind of ritual in the basement, and now he's getting her fired. Point six, who captured Kyle down there in that crypt, and who gave the order to *get rid of him*?"

"I think it was my science teacher," Kyle mumbled.

Everyone turned to stare at him.

"Your science teacher?" Mallory asked, astounded.

Kyle pushed his cracked glasses farther up on his nose. "Yeah, Mr. Parsell."

"From what I know about Selwyn Parsell, he's nothing but a big old teddy bear!" exclaimed Aggie. "Why would you think he has anything to do with what's going on in the museum?"

"Because I've seen the way he looks at me whenever I challenge him on the laws of physics."

"Good grief, Kyle," Mallory groaned. "I challenge him, too. That's what students are supposed to do."

"Yeah, but I've seen him give me the *evil eye* when he thinks

I'm not looking," Kyle grumbled.

Aggie sat back in her seat to look at Mallory. "Then you'd better be careful, Mal. Mr. Parsell may try to get rid of you as well," she teased.

Ignoring her grandmother, Mallory resumed reading her notes. "Okay, point number seven, who locked the basement door?"

"And more importantly, who unlocked it?" Victoria added.

"Right," said Mallory, scribbling in her notepad.

"Whoever unlocked the door is obviously on your side, Mallory," Ron said, "but I wonder why they didn't identify themself?"

"And that's what makes this whole situation even weirder," Mallory frowned.

"Any more points, granddaughter?" Aggie asked.

"Number eight, Nathifa's strange story about something preventing her from meeting her Prince in the afterlife."

"Personally, I think that's the oddest point of all," Aggie said. "Can't even begin to fathom out what's going on there."

Mallory tucked her pencil behind her ear and looked up. "Those are all the major points so far."

"And none of them make any sense," Kyle sighed

"All the more reason why I think Mallory and I should go back to the museum and search the basement–" Aggie broke off as the bell at the front door began to tinkle. "We'll figure out when we'll do this and let the rest of you know," she whispered as she stood to greet the two customers entering the teashop.

Chapter 23

Mallory followed her grandmother up the Midville Museum steps, tugging in annoyance at the long blonde wig jammed tightly on her head and wondering for the umpteenth time why she had ever agreed to wear such an absurd outfit.

"I thought we were trying not to be noticed," she grumbled.

"This is not about not being noticed," Aggie said, glancing back at her granddaughter. "It's about not being recognized." Hunched over her wooden cane Aggie looked every bit the fragile elderly woman as she shuffled her way through the museum's front doors.

Aggie had found herself a grey-haired wig, pince-nez glasses, striped cotton blouse, shapeless green cardigan, and waist-high skirt. As a final touch to her garish ensemble, she had added a cheap silk scarf and a chunky red plastic necklace.

She's having way too much fun, Mallory thought grumpily as she tugged on the pleated plaid skirt Aggie insisted she wear. Along with the short skirt was a horrid over-sized blue blazer, and a pair of scuffed up black-and-white saddle shoes. As far as Mallory was concerned, she looked even more ridiculous than Aggie.

And standing in the foyer watching the odd pair approaching the Egyptian entrance, Eleanor Snodgrass thought the same thing.

"Unfortunately you've arrived too late for a tour of the exhibit," she called out.

"Oh, that's quite all right, my dear," Aggie said in her best quivering old lady voice. "My name is, "Mrs. Hob . . . son. Yes, Julia Hobson. Just thought my niece and I would stroll around a bit before the museum closes. We can come back again tomorrow for the tour."

Miss Snodgrass shrugged indifferently then turned and walked over to join a short man standing at the far side of the gallery.

"That was Eleanor Snodgrass," Mallory whispered to Aggie. "And the man she's now standing with is Mortimus Claxley."

"Snodgrass and Claxley, huh?" Aggie glanced casually over her shoulder. "Yup, they look as untrustworthy as I imagined them to be." Saying nothing more, she spun around in her laced-up granny shoes and toddled off toward the tomb entrance.

Mallory continued to study the docent and curator whose conversation soon escalated into a heated debate. When Miss Snodgrass glanced her way, Mallory, worried the stern woman might recognize her so she quickly followed after her grandmother through the tomb entrance.

For the next twenty minutes, Aggie walked around the gallery showing genuine interest in all the Egyptian displays and ancient artifacts. Mallory trailed behind, keeping an eye out for anything suspicious. When the staff announced the closing of the museum, they both made for the mummy's room and crouched down behind the sarcophagus. Familiar with the routine, Mallory waited until the last of the visitors and staff had exited the building and the security lights had been turned on before she stood up. Aggie rose up beside her, sighing in relief as she rubbed the circulation back into her arms and legs.

"Hate to admit it, but I just may be getting too old for this kind of thing," she mumbled.

"You, Aggie? Never," Mallory said, working just as hard to get the kinks out of her own limbs.

Before long they were creeping past the looming warrior statues and gold chariot. Once they reached the basement sign they followed the narrow staircase downwards and stepped into the dark crypt.

"Okay, you start searching for the statue on that side and I'll start this side," Aggie said, turning on her flashlight. "Make sure you look under every nook and cranny and whatever you do, don't tell me if you run across any snakes. I don't want to know."

They had barely begun their search when to their horror they heard the sound of heavy footsteps coming down the staircase. Mallory grabbed Aggie and pulled her back behind a stack of boxes. They had barely switched off their flashlights when two individuals clad in black hooded robes crept into the basement, the second one carrying a small wooden chest. After placing the chest on the workbench they pushed the cowls back from their head. Mallory stifled a gasp. There stood Mortimus Claxley, the museum curator. But to Mallory's surprise the other hooded individual was not, as Mallory had expected, Miss Snodgrass. It was a man she did not recognize.

The accomplice stepped forward. "What makes you think the statue is here?" he asked the curator.

"I don't, but if that statue is anywhere in this museum, my spell will bring it out of its hiding place," Claxley hissed.

Working silently, Claxley opened the chest lid and lifted out the curious-looking manuscript Kyle had described. The strange gold design on the cover seemed to glow with a light of its own. He also removed a set of black candlesticks and a small brass container and placed them on the workbench next to the open book. Pulling the hood back over his head he lit the candles and opened the manuscript. His partner struck a match and plunged it into the small brass container. Within minutes a swirl of black smoke plumed up from its center, filling the basement with the pungent smell of incense.

The arcane priest began reciting a series of odd-sounding words and as his voice rose in intensity, a vaporous green light began to spiral up from the center of the book, reflecting eerily off the nearby walls. The hypnotic chant continued and soon the other individual, with his hood back over his head, joined in. The air turned heavy and oppressive and Mallory began to feel weak and dizzy. Odd shuffling noises drifted up from the darkened corridor and a number of items fell from the shelves as the mesmerizing chant continued. And then, as if on cue, the two hooded individuals stopped, threw their cowls back, and spun around, scanning the depths of the dark crypt as the wispy green light swirled back into the book,

"Guess it didn't work, Master," the other man finally whispered.

"I can see that, you idiot."

"Are you sure it was the right activation spell?"

"Yes, it was the right one," Claxley snarled. "If the ushabti didn't make its appearance it means it's not here. Jarman must have taken it home with him."

"Remind me again why this particular statue is so important to you."

Claxley slammed the book closed. "Because I've figured out there's a connection between that ushabti and the Egyptian mummy upstairs. The hieroglyphics on the sarcophagus say that a piece of jewelry was placed on the muse's body at the time of her burial, but x-rays done some years ago showed no jewelry under the linen wrappings."

"Okay, but what does that have to do with the statue?"

Claxley's sigh was filled with exasperation. "Listen up because I'm only going to explain it to you once. After the Egyptian exhibit arrived and that ushabti started moving, it wasn't hard to figure out it was probably being triggered by some kind of magic attached to the exhibit."

"And?"

"I believe the ushabti can give us a clue where to find this valuable piece of jewelry and if we can find it, I know a private collector who will pay a staggering fortune for it."

"So if that statue was here in the museum, the initiating spell would have made it appear, right?"

"Yes," grunted Mortimus Claxley impatiently. He snuffed out the candles, capped the incense holder and stepped back to let his accomplice return the items to the chest. Within minutes the pair had grabbed everything and disappeared up the stairs out of sight.

Mallory and Aggie waited an agonizing ten minutes before easing themselves out from their place of concealment.

"So, that's why he's after that ushabti," Aggie mused. "He thinks it'll lead him to a valuable piece of jewelry."

Mallory sighed with disappointment. "But obviously the statue isn't here in the museum, is it?"

"Don't be so sure, child," Aggie said, her eyes glinting mischievously in the beam of her flashlight. "I believe I may know exactly where that statue is hidden. Exactly."

Mallory gaped at Aggie. Had the incense befuddled her thinking? "Okay, then, where is it?" she asked.

"Here."

"Here where?"

"In the basement."

"Look Aggie, if magic couldn't find the statue, why do you think you know where it is?"

Aggie pointed to the box she'd been hiding behind. "Pretty sure it's in there. I was leaning on the top trying to watch those two do all their weird stuff when I felt the lid vibrate."

"As if something was trying to get out," Mallory gasped. Her eyes grew wide with excitement.

"Exactly," Aggie continued. "Once I realized what was going on, I leaned even harder on the lid. No way those two were going to get that statue, not to mention if they heard the noise, we would have been discovered."

Mallory grabbed the lid to the box and lifted it up. There on a pile of packing material lay a twelve-inch high bright blue statue. Aggie carefully picked it up, studied it for a moment then stuffed it in her over-sized purse.

"Now let's get out of here," she said, heading swiftly for the staircase.

Mallory followed her grandmother, hoping they would be able to sneak out of the museum without being seen. When they reached the top step, Aggie leaned back to whisper, "Get in front, Mallory, your eyes are better than mine. Make sure the way is clear then we'll make a run for it."

Make a run for it? Mallory stared at Aggie in dismay. Run was not something she'd ever seen her grandmother do, let alone do in a pair of thick-heeled granny shoes. Easing past her, Mallory peered into the shadowed museum. Hearing nothing, she crept forward. Aggie followed and soon they were inching their way toward the front doors, but as they pushed at the emergency exit bar and slipped through the opening an alarm immediately sounded behind them.

"Okay, this is when we run!" Aggie shouted, and took off down the steps.

Once on the street they found Lorna's hidden car and after jumping in, hightailed it from the area. It was not until they reached the main highway heading toward Cedar Creek that Aggie eased back on the accelerator and leaned back in her seat with a laugh.

"Haven't had this much fun in years," she guffawed. "We've got to do it again sometime."

"I thought you said you were getting too old for this kind of thing," Mallory reminded her.

Ignoring her granddaughter's statement, Aggie rambled on. "Here's what I think we should do next. Call a team meeting and show them what we've found."

"Good idea," Mallory agreed. "I'll alert everyone to meet at the teashop tomorrow."

"Meantime," Aggie continued, "I'll keep the statue locked up in my personal safe. If it tries to move, it won't go far. My security box is anchored safely to the floor."

Mallory settled back in the seat. A moment later her eyes came to rest on her scuffed up saddle shoes. They really do look ridiculous, she thought, and was soon laughing as raucously as her grandmother.

Chapter 25

Ron was out with friends when Mallory returned home that night so she could not tell him what had happened at the museum. Weary and exhausted, she ate a quick dinner, said goodnight to her mother, and climbed the stairs to bed. She had hardly crawled between the sheets when she noticed a familiar red glow moving along the wall toward her.

Leaping from the bed, she crossed to the standing oval mirror and waited as the surface filled with swirling white mist. Soon the distant sounds of children and barking dogs drifted into the room as the image of the River Nile with its sweeping dunes of wind-rippled sand materialized on the glass. When Nathifa's barge drew into sight the excited young woman stepped forward, followed by her Nubian handmaiden, Halima.

"Mal-lor-ree, I thank the gods we are able to meet again!" she cried. "I know you have found something for I sense its nearness."

"You mean the ushabti?" Mallory asked.

"If that is what it is, then I believe it holds the answer to that which will set me free."

"Well, I'm not sure how," Mallory said, somewhat frustrated that she had so little to offer Nathifa. "We're meeting tomorrow to see if we can figure out why this statue is so important to everyone.

Hopefully we'll discover how it might help. Meantime, any clues on what to look for?"

"No," the muse said, her shoulders sagging. "I sense nothing else." She stopped for a moment as Halima leaned over to whisper in her ear.

"My handmaiden suggests you simply return the statue to me," Nathifa added.

"You mean here? In my room?"

"No, to where my body lies."

Mallory gasped. "Back where . . . in the sarcoph . . . with your dead–" she broke off, uncomfortable at the thought.

"Yes," said Nathifa.

Mallory sighed, loud and deep. "I don't know how that will help, but if that's what we have to do to set you free, I promise we'll get it back to you."

Halima breathed a sigh of relief. Until this strange spell was broken, she was as trapped as Nathifa. Within minutes the image began to dissipate, along with the red glow on the wall. Mallory called a quick goodbye and after the mirror returned to normal, hurried back to her bed. But her thoughts were heavy. Would they have time to solve the mystery before the Egyptian exhibit was shipped back to the Museum of Cairo?

When the group gathered the following day at the teashop, Aggie described her adventure with Mallory and what they had overheard in the basement. After checking no one was spying on them through the plate glass window, Aggie withdrew the ushabti from her purse and stood it in the center of the table. No one said a word. They just stared in silent wonder at the shiny female statue with its identifiable Egyptian headpiece and crossed arms.

"If you're waiting for it to move," Mallory whispered, "it

probably won't if we're all watching it."

Aggie shook her head. "Probably not."

Kyle picked up the statue and shook it hard.

"Kyle, what are you doing?" Victoria asked, concerned. "That's a valuable item."

"I was wondering if there might be a piece of paper or something hidden inside with a spell to undo whatever has Nathifa trapped in her strange world."

"Good thought, Kyle," Ron said, "but even if the statue is hollow, I doubt a note inside would still be readable after this many years."

"Kyle might be on to something though," Mallory said, her eyes narrow in thought.

"But statues like this are usually solid," Victoria added.

"How about drilling a hole on the bottom and finding out," Kyle suggested.

Victoria continued to look aghast. "Drilling into a valuable artifact?"

Mallory pondered their predicament then jumped up and headed for the counter. "I'm going to call Mrs. Danner. I need to ask her a couple of things," she called back. Grabbing the phone, Mallory slid down behind the counter out of earshot. A few minutes later, she returned to the table and slipped back into her seat.

"Okay, here's the scoop on the ushabti," she said. "According to Mrs. Danner, the statue was donated to the museum ten years ago after the death of a man who collected Egyptian antiquities. He apparently bought it from someone around the turn of the century. She said it had never moved in all the years it had been on display at Midville, and that it's made out of a material called faience. Even though it's probably thousands of years old, this particular ushabti doesn't have a huge price tag because there are so many like it in museums and collections throughout the world."

"Faience . . ." Ron murmured, thumbing through his dictionary. "Okay, listen to this. Faience was a paste made of ground quartz, or made with sand that had a high percentage of quartz. The faience paste was pressed into molds and then fired. When baked, the glaze would migrate to the outside producing a smooth glassy surface. The quality and color of the glaze depended on the impurities in the paste. A faience ushabti ranged in color from bright dark blue to various shades of turquoise and pale green."

"Cool," said Kyle.

"I also asked Mrs. Danner if she thought the statue might be hollow," Mallory added. "She didn't know, but she said some Egyptologists x-ray mummies and items of antiquity to see what might be inside them."

"Yes!" Aggie cried excitedly. "We heard Claxley say it wasn't until after they x-rayed the mummy that they learned she wasn't wearing the necklace mentioned in the hieroglyphics."

"So, let's x-ray the ushabti then," said Kyle.

Everyone turned to Aggie, as if she would have the answer. She stared out pensively for a moment then gave a mischievous grin. "Hmm, now that I think about it, I do believe our local radiologist may owe me a favor."

Pleased at remembering this, Aggie packed the statue back in her purse and stood to leave. "Watch the shop until I get back," she instructed Mallory, and then marched toward the door. It banged shut behind her.

"That woman works fast, doesn't she?" Kyle said, gazing after Aggie with a look of pure admiration.

Chapter 26

By the time Aggie strode back into the teashop the shades had been drawn and the sign on the door turned to 'Closed', but Mallory, Kyle, Victoria, and Ron were sitting waiting for her.

"Glad you're still here," Aggie said with a grin. She sat down and pulled the statue from her purse. "Guess I cashed in my favor a while back so I had to promise Joe a month of cream puffs. It was worth it though," she said, and slapped an x-ray down next to the ushabti. "The statue is hollow and there's definitely something hidden inside it."

Mallory grabbed the x-ray, squinting to make out the shadowy object inside. "Then we have no choice but to open it up," she said, pushing the x-ray toward Victoria. "Whatever this is could be the very thing Nathifa needs to get free."

Victoria studied the x-ray and nodded slowly. "I guess Kyle's idea of drilling out the bottom will have to be done."

Ron turned to ask his grandmother if she might have something they could use, but Aggie had already scooted from the table and was heading for her toolbox. She returned carrying an armful of gadgets, including a small portable drill and a cloth to work with on the table. She looked around, waiting for someone to volunteer to do it.

"Well?" Aggie finally asked.

"Oh, all right," Kyle sighed. "After all it was my suggestion."

He grabbed the statue, picked up the drill and turned it on. The small bit whirred into action and before long the table was covered in a layer of fine powdery dust. When the hole was large enough, Kyle grabbed a pair of small pliers and carefully pulled out the object stuffed tightly inside. He placed the item, which was wrapped in a piece of age-yellowed cloth, onto the table then gestured for Mallory to open it up. Within moments they were all peering at an ornate silver necklace set with rubies, red carnelian, and cobalt blue lapis lazuli stones.

"Look at that!" Victoria gasped as the stones in the necklace sparkled beneath the overhead light.

"It's gorgeous," Mallory whispered.

"It looks like the one painted on Nathifa's coffin," Kyle noted.

The tearoom went quiet until Aggie spoke. "Okay, now that we have this little beauty, what are we supposed to do with it?"

Mallory gently picked up the necklace, her brow furrowed. "Well, obviously we have to get this back to Nathifa, although we still don't know how it's going to help get her to the Underworld."

"Maybe she'll appear again tonight and tell you," Kyle said.

"Maybe," Mallory mumbled, "but if she doesn't, then we'll have to figure it out for ourselves."

They fell silent again until Mallory spoke. "I think I have an idea."

"Knew you'd get there sooner or later," Aggie nodded, relief in her voice. "Fire away, dear."

"We simply return the necklace to Nathifa in the coffin."

"And then what?" Kyle asked.

"I don't know," Mallory shrugged. "I only know it's

important to get this back to her."

"I agree," Aggie said, her face serious, "but anyone could take it if they see it in the coffin, not to mention that greedy Mortimus Claxley or Miss Snodgrass could recognize us if we try to get back in the museum again."

"Well, there's more to my idea," Mallory continued, turning to Aggie. "Where's that fake necklace you were wearing yesterday?"

Aggie rummaged through her purse, pulled out the cheap costume jewelry, and placed it on the table.

"Perfect," Mallory muttered as she picked it up and wrapped it in the original frayed piece of yellowed cloth. "The only way to get Claxley off our tail so we can return the real necklace to the sarcophagus," she explained, stuffing everything back inside the statue, "is to reseal the ushabti with this, and then set it up so that he finds it. We'll hide it in one of the skulls inside the basement late Saturday afternoon."

"I'm sure you've already thought this out, but how will he know it's there?" Ron asked.

"He'll know because we'll have Mrs. Danner casually drop the hint that she's just found out where Mr. Jarman hid the statue. Which, of course, will be where we've hidden it. She will also suggest that the statue should be x-rayed to find out why it keeps moving."

Kyle bounced from his seat in excitement. "I can see it now. After Claxley discovers the statue, he'll have to wait until Monday to get it x-rayed. By that time the exhibit will be packed up, and hopefully, on its way back to Egypt."

"And Nathifa on her way to the afterlife," Aggie muttered.

"That plan might just work, Mallory!" Ron cried. "And because Victoria and I haven't been to the museum and won't be recognized by anyone, I think we should go and hide it there."

"My thoughts exactly," Mallory said as she stood the statue back on its base.

"I'll buy some plaster and blue paint tomorrow to reseal the bottom of that," Aggie said, pointing to the ushabti. "It can spend the rest of the day drying, and then be ready for Ron and Victoria to take with them."

"And I'll call Mrs. Danner tonight and tell her what we want Claxley to overhear," Mallory said. "Hopefully she'll go along with our plan."

"Fine. In the meantime, let's keep quiet about all this," Aggie cautioned. She glanced furtively over her shoulder before continuing. "The last thing we need is for our local Police Chief to come snooping around here asking more questions."

Chapter 21

"That looks perfect!" Mallory exclaimed. "Like it's been that way for centuries."

It was Saturday morning and everyone stood admiring the patched ushabti statue in Aggie's teashop.

"I talked with Mrs. Danner," Mallory said, "and she's ready to go along with my idea. She thought it was very strange, but I promised her we'd explain it all later."

Ron wrapped the ancient relic in a thick cloth and placed it carefully in his backpack. "Once the statue is hidden," he said, "we'll find Mrs. Danner and let her know to go ahead and drop the hint to Claxley."

An hour later Victoria watched from the top of Midville Museum's basement stairs as Ron raced down into its dark depths. He reappeared a few minutes later, flashing Victoria a thumb's up and wearing a grin of success. Together they returned to the main floor and slipped unnoticed into the crowd. When Mrs. Danner appeared in the corridor from her office, Victoria ambled casually over to tell her they were ready to put the rest of their plan into motion, Victoria and Ron left the museum soon after and biked back to Cedar Creek.

"Mission accomplished," Ron said when they returned to the

teashop. "I stuffed the statue up tightly inside one of the skulls so Claxley won't have a problem believing it had no way of getting out the night of his magical ritual."

"And Mrs. Danner said she'd call and let us know when he takes the bait," Victoria added.

"Let's keep our fingers crossed until then," Mallory sighed.

"Wonder how long that'll be," Aggie grumbled. Her chair scraped harshly on the floor as she stood to trudge to the back of the teashop mumbling all the way about how hard it was to sit and wait.

"When you think about Nathifa waiting thousands of years," Mallory called after her, "what's a couple more hours?"

"Like a couple hundred years," Aggie shouted back.

"That woman has no patience," Mallory said to no one in particular as she straightened the chair beside her.

It was late in the day when Mrs. Danner called the teashop.

"Okay," Aggie said after hanging up. "Here's how it went down. Emily Danner said she knew Claxley had overheard her whisper the information to another employee because right after that, he turned and hurried off toward the basement. He has now disappeared from the museum, along with the security guard he hired."

"Great, if Claxley and his guard have gone for good it will be easier for us to get back in the museum tomorrow," Mallory said. "All we have to do is figure out what to do with the real necklace once we get there."

"I know you told us Nathifa didn't appear last night," Kyle grunted, "but let's hope she comes tonight."

"But if she doesn't . . ." Ron hesitated . . ."then what?"

"No point in worrying about it now," Aggie said. "We'll just have to wait and see, won't we?"

Mallory's eyes widened. Was this statement coming from a woman who has trouble waiting? Still she had to admit, Aggie was right. Waiting, it seemed, was all they could do.

"She didn't appear," Mallory called to tell Aggie the following morning. "No red glow, no sand on the floor, no image in the mirror. Nada."

"Then do you have any more good ideas?" Aggie asked. "This is the last day before the exhibit goes back to Egypt, you know."

Mallory sighed.

"All right," Aggie said, "Call everybody in for another pow-wow. Maybe as a group we can decide on a course of action."

Within a half hour the team had gathered in *Ye Olde Tea Shoppe*, anxious and confused.

"I think we should just put the necklace in the coffin," Kyle said, pulling out a chair and slumping into it.

Mallory shook her head. "Somebody could take it if they saw it lying there."

"Then how about we unwind some of that wrapping, lay it on Nathifa's body, and wrap her up again," Kyle continued.

Victoria's eyes widened in alarm, "Heavens, no! Unwrapping a mummy would be like desecrating a national treasure."

"And there's no guarantee it will help anyway," Ron added.

After they tossed around a few more suggestions, Aggie rose from her seat. "Well, time is running out and I think we should get over to the museum. If we get any brainwaves while we're there, at least we'll be close enough to actually do something."

Within minutes everyone had piled into Aggie's VW van. They arrived in Midville a short time later and hurried up the museum steps. The last day of the exhibit had been opened up free to the public and the foyer was crowded with visitors. Aggie skirted around the sightseers and led the way to the mummy's room, but to their horror, when they got there, they found the door locked. A sign in front stated that the last showing of the sarcophagus had been a half hour earlier.

"You're too late," a recognizable voice snapped behind them.

Mallory turned to find Eleanor Snodgrass eyeing them coldly.

"They're about to pack everything up in the mummy room so no one is permitted to enter," she said bluntly. With no further concern, she tossed her head and strode off to join the sightseers coming through the tomb entrance.

"Any thoughts on what to do next?" Mallory asked.

"You mean other than breaking into the mummy room?" Kyle asked.

"Well, normally I would not encourage anyone to break into a locked room," Aggie said, "but we are rather desperate–" she broke off in disbelief at the figure striding toward them.

Cedar Creek's Chief of Police came to a stop scrutinizing each in turn. "Didn't expect to find you all here today," he said, his eyes narrow with suspicion.

"Nice to see you, too, John," Aggie said, matter-of-factly. "What brings you to Midville?"

"Thought I might catch the exhibit before it leaves."

"Thought the same thing ourselves," Aggie nodded.

John Banks looked over at the mummy room. "And you are all standing outside this closed room because . . . ?"

"Because we're trying to decide where to go next," Aggie grunted impatiently.

The Chief paused for a moment then turned to walk away. "In case you need anything," he called warningly over his shoulder, "I'll be here for a while keeping an eye on things."

Mallory swallowed hard. John Banks hovering in the background could make things sticky, especially if they tried to break into the mummy room. And if that wasn't bad enough, Mallory saw another familiar figure approaching. It was the strange costumed guard. But wasn't he supposed to have disappeared with Claxley? Before Mallory could wonder further, the guard raised his arm and pointed his spear at the mummy room. She watched puzzled as he then backed into the shadowed corridor and disappeared. Mallory shook her head. That man gets stranger and stranger.

But to her astonishment, the door to the mummy's room began to swing open.

"Whoa! Looks like Egyptian magic is at it again," Kyle cried and rushed forward. The rest of the group followed. Once inside the room, they secured the door behind them. Musty smelling packing crates sat waiting to be filled in the dimly lit room, but thankfully the smaller Egyptian coffin containing the mummy still sat open on its pedestal.

Now what?" Kyle whispered to Mallory.

But before she could answer, a low hollow growl suddenly echoed through the room. To Kyle's horror, the wooden statue of Anubis turned its head and stared at him, its kohl lined eyes flashing brilliant yellow.

"Please tell me that's not happening," Kyle groaned, staggering backwards.

Anubis growled a second time and then music, faint as a

whisper, began to drift up from the sarcophagus. A jolt of electrical energy rushed through Mallory and the hair on her arms rose up. As if in a trance she reached for Aggie's purse, removed the necklace, and walked toward the coffin. She placed the amulet around the muse's neck and stood back. The necklace, shimmering in a kaleidoscope of radiant colors began to ripple through the wrappings. Within seconds it had completely disappeared from sight.

On the ride back to Cedar Creek, the conversation never left the subject of what had happened in the mummy room.

"Kyle, why did you go all crazy when we first went in there?" Ron asked.

Kyle shivered. "It was that jackal dog. It freaked me out when it turned its head and glared at me."

"Turned its head?' Ron said. "I didn't see it do that."

"You didn't hear it growl?"

"Nope, didn't hear it growl either."

"And I didn't see Anubis move," Victoria added. "How about you, Aggie?"

"Can't say as I did."

"Nobody else saw what happened?" Kyle spluttered.

Mallory shook her head.

"Dad keeps saying I have an over-active imagination," Kyle frowned. "Maybe I just *thought* I saw it."

"Maybe not," Aggie said. "There was definitely some weird magic going on in that room today, and who knows, maybe you're even developing psychic gifts like Mallory."

"I hope not," Kyle mumbled. "One paranormal detective is enough in Cedar Creek."

Although everyone else laughed, Mallory sat quiet, deep in thought. With the exhibit leaving the museum the following day, she wondered how would they ever find out if Nathifa had been helped.

An hour later, Aggie dropped Mallory and Ron off outside their cottage. Tired and weary, Mallory climbed the stairs to her room and once in bed, fell fast asleep.

She awoke a short time later to the sound of a distant flute. Rubbing the sleep from her eyes she scurried excitedly across the floor, her heart pounding as she stood before the oval mirror.

Soon the Egyptian barge sailed into view. Mallory's heart beat even faster as the boat, decorated with long tendrils of colored ribbons, pulled to shore. A tall handsome man wearing a royal kilt and the headpiece of a Pharaoh stepped forward.

Nathifa stood beside him wearing the necklace Mallory had placed on her mummified body earlier that day.

"I cannot thank you enough for your help, my young friend," Nathifa said, her smile wide. "It has enabled me to finally join my Prince."

Mallory could hardly breathe. A Pharaoh from ancient Egypt was in her room! The handsome bronze-skinned man gave a slight bow. "I have heard much about you, Mal-lor-ree," he said, his voice soft. "I wish to thank you and all who helped free Nathifa from her entrapment."

"You're welcome," Mallory replied, unsure whether she should bow back to this regal man or not. "But how did Nathifa get caught in that strange world in the first place?"

"I will explain," the Prince said. "After my love died, I did not trust the temple priests to prepare her body correctly for the journey she was about to make. I even suspected they were the ones responsible for poisoning her. To be certain Nathifa would be in the Promised Land when it was time for me to journey there, I had a special necklace made for her. Unbeknownst to anyone, I placed a spell on it to safeguard her until after she reached the afterlife.

"Unfortunately, one of the men preparing her body for burial decided the necklace would have more value in his possession than in a tomb," the Prince continued. "Before wrapping her body for the funerary services, he removed the necklace, and after hollowing out an ushabti statue, stuffed the amulet inside. When he left that night he took the statue with him–"

"I have since learned that because they buried me without the necklace," Nathifa interrupted, "the spell could not be activated to protect and guide me onwards. That is why I became caught in the World Between Worlds."

The Prince continued. "But the gods saw fit to punish the man for stealing the necklace. On his way home that night he was accosted by thieves and killed. The robbers took the statue, unaware of the treasure hidden inside." The Prince paused and shook his head puzzled. "Unfortunately, I do not know what happened to the ushabti after it was stolen."

Mallory stepped closer. "I think I may know the rest of the story your highness . . . um, pharaoh-ship . . . um–" She looked at him apologetically. With a slight smile the Prince beckoned her to continue.

"Well, thousands of years after all this happened," Mallory began, "the statue found its way to my country where a private collector of antiquities purchased it. Of course he didn't know there was a necklace hidden inside the ushabti. Anyway, after this man's death, his collection was given to the Midville Museum."

"Nathifa has spoken to me of this museum," the Prince said,

leaning forward with his eyes bright and intense at what he was hearing. "Please tell me more."

"I guess most of this man's collection got stored in the museum basement until someone could find time to catalogue everything," Mallory continued. "But a few pieces found their way into the museum, and the ushabti statue was one of them—"

She stopped abruptly to stare in disbelief toward the rear of the barque. A familiar looking man stood there, his black hair cut in bangs. He wore a white linen wrap, a matching cape, and leather thongs.

Mallory peered closer. "That's the guard I kept running into in the museum," she gasped. "So, that's why nobody else could see him. He's from the ancient past, isn't he?"

Nathifa nodded. "Yes, this is Ini-Herit. He was assigned by the royal Prince to protect me on my journey to the afterlife."

"And he got stuck in the same place you did when the necklace was stolen," Mallory finished.

Nathifa looked back sadly at Ini-Herit and nodded.

"And was it also Ini-Herit who unlocked the door for Kyle and me that night when we were locked in the basement?"

Nathifa nodded again.

"So, let me get this straight," Mallory said. "It wasn't until the Egyptian exhibit arrived at the museum that the spell in the ushabti got activated and started moving on the museum shelf, right?"

"Yes," spoke the Prince. "Under the right conditions, it has the ability to step out of time and space and move at will."

"And that's when Mortimus Claxley figured out the moving statue had to be linked to the exhibit," murmured to herself.

The guard moved forward on the barge as Nathifa explained further. "The rituals your arcane priest conducted released my loyal protector and messenger, Ini-Herit to carry out his assignment. He first appeared to you as a scarab."

"Right," Mallory said with a half-grin. "A scarab that could talk."

Nathifa laughed. "He thought it best to take on that form rather than appear as himself."

"Okay, so why did that statue of the jackal god blink at me?" Mallory asked.

"Anubis is known in your history as the jackal god, but in my time we called him Horus–"

"Horus!" Mallory exclaimed.

"Yes, a god who protects the dead. It was not until the protection spell on the necklace was invoked that he was able to help me."

At that moment Mallory's attention fell on Halima standing quietly in the background.

Nathifa turned to smile at the tall Nubian girl. "Halima has also been released from this spell," she explained, "but she wishes to stay and serve me in the afterlife."

Before Mallory could say more, waves of hot desert air gusted from the mirror sweeping urgently into the room.

"I fear we must go," Nathifa cried, her voice rising above a cacophony of distant bells. "Thank you for helping me, Mal-lor-ree. I hope we can meet again some day."

Mallory watched helplessly as the barge backed swiftly from the shore and turned to head for the middle of the river. "Nathifa, wait!" she called out desperately. "There's so much I wanted to ask you, like who built the great pyramid, and the sphinx?"

Nathifa's voice echoed back faintly across the river. "It is not one sphinx but two that guard the great pyramid."

"Two sphinxes?"

"Beneath the sands . . . they . . . will . . . discover . . . this . . . soon–"

Nathifa's voice ended abruptly as the image in the mirror spiraled into a circle and disappeared in a burst of white light.

Mallory stood staring at the empty mirror for a while longer, then returned to her bed, saddened at the thought she might never see Nathifa again. She lay for a long time going over every detail of her conversation with Nathifa and the Prince, but then, too weary to wonder what everyone would think once she told them about the second sphinx buried in the sands of Egypt, closed her eyes and fell into a thankful dreamless sleep.

Chapter 30

The following morning, after dressing for school, Mallory ran down the stairs and into the kitchen.

"Oh, there you are," her mother said, reaching for a small wrapped package sitting on the table beside her. "This came Special Delivery for you this morning."

Munching on the last of her waffles, Lorna watched curiously as Mallory opened the box and looked inside. There, covered in soft cotton, lay a silver armband set with a red carnelian scarab beetle surrounded by small blue stones. Stunned at such a beautiful gift, Mallory lifted it carefully from the box. A note stuffed beneath it fell to the table.

Hi Mallory,

I found this in a strange little antique shop a few days ago and felt compelled to purchase it for you. I have a feeling it's very old, could even be from ancient Egypt. Don't know how it landed in that shop, but I just couldn't seem to leave without buying it. Hope you enjoy it.

Kevin

"What a lovely thought!" Lorna exclaimed. "You must be sure to thank Kevin."

"I will Mom," Mallory nodded. "I'll write him tonight." Unexpectedly, a warmth as gentle as a desert breeze brushed across her face.

"Are you all right?" her mother asked.

"Yes, why?"

"You went a little pale just then."

"Probably need something to eat," Mallory mumbled, still conscious of the warm caress.

Lorna handed Mallory a plate of waffles, eyeing her closely.

"I'm okay, Mom, honestly," Mallory reassured her.

"All right, I'll take your word for it." Lorna frowned, concerned at her daughter's odd behavior. She eased on a pair of black high heels, grabbed her purse, and turned to leave. "Call me at work if you don't feel good at school. I'll come and get you right away." She headed for the front door.

Mallory nodded then grabbed her fork and began to eat. After rinsing her empty plate, she called her grandmother. "Aggie?"

"The one and only," Aggie grunted. "What's up?"

"Nathifa came back last night."

"Good, I hoped she might." Aggie sounded pleased.

"I have things to tell everyone, but can we all meet at your house when you get home from the teashop later? I have some homework I really need to finish first."

Aggie grunted again. "Don't see why not, unless I can't wait that long to hear what you have to say." She paused before adding, "Now that I think about it though, it's probably a good idea to do it later. I'd like to talk with Emily Danner first about what went on after we left the museum yesterday."

"Good, I'll see you then." Mallory hung up the phone and returned the armband to the box. She couldn't wait to show everyone Kevin's gift.

Kyle apparently got the time and meeting place wrong after school let out and turned up at Aggie's teashop instead.

"If I didn't know better," Aggie said, her eyes narrow with suspicion as she handed him a slice of hot quiche pie. "I'd say that was a convenient mistake."

"Thanks, Aggie." Kyle gave a sly grin. He hadn't forgotten quiche was always served on Mondays. He took the plate and headed for the nearest table. "I talked with Mallory at school," he called back. "Said she wanted to wait until we were all together to tell us what happened last night. Sounded pretty excited about sharing whatever it was though."

"Yup, I got that impression, too."

Before Aggie or Kyle could say more, the bell on the front door jingled.

Aggie looked up then groaned quietly. "Now what?"

Heavy steps sounded on the wood floor as John Banks stomped in their direction.

"Afternoon, Aggie," he nodded. "Kyle."

"Afternoon, sir," Kyle replied, his mouth full.

"Like some tea, John?" Aggie asked.

"Not right now, thanks Aggie," the stern man said. "Thought you might like to know that the Midville Police called me a short while ago. Seems like one of Midville Museum's senior curators called Mortimus Claxley, and a guard he hired, have absconded with a valuable artifact. Seems also that this curator has been trying to pin some other missing museum pieces on Emily Danner. The museum was about to let her go, you know."

"Yes, I did hear that." Aggie studied the chief curiously.

"Well, they found those missing pieces hidden in Claxley's office," he continued.

"No kidding!" Kyle exclaimed. "In his office?"

John Banks turned to study Kyle before answering. "Yes, but now that this has come to light, Emily is being reinstated back on the staff with Mr. Jarman's deepest apologies. He's the head of the museum, you know."

"Yes, I do believe I was aware of that, too." Aggie's face was the usual picture of innocence.

"Has Mr. Claxley been arrested?" Kyle asked.

"Not yet. Seems neither he nor the guard can be found."

"Rotten scoundrels, that's all I have to say about those two," Aggie mumbled, annoyed.

Kyle nodded furiously.

John Banks's eyes slid from one to the other, puzzled at their intense reaction to the news of the two missing thieves. "Well, just thought you'd be interested in knowing what's going on," he added. "After all I must admit I did for a little while think your group might have had something to do with all the problems going on over there at Midville Museum. Guess I was wrong."

"Seems you were, John," Aggie agreed sweetly. "But don't give it another thought. Being wrong can happen to the best of us." She resumed wiping the glass counter as the Sheriff turned to leave.

"You have a good day now, Chief," Aggie called as he exited through the door.

Chapter 31

Later that day after everyone had gathered in Aggie's cozy kitchen, Mallory relayed her account of Nathifa's return the night before.

"You should have seen that Prince." Mallory swooned toward Victoria. "He was sooo tall and handsome."

"Let's not forget he's centuries old, Mallory," Kyle said bitingly.

Mallory ignored him and continued her story about Nathifa wearing the necklace, and about the Prince's spell of protection that had backfired.

"And here's another thing," Mallory said, pulling Smothers the cat onto her lap and stroking his silky fur. "That guard I kept seeing in the museum was assigned by the Prince to protect Nathifa. That's why I was the only one who could ever see him. He was also the one who unlocked the basement door for Kyle and me that night in the museum."

"You're saying that the costumed guard wasn't the one Claxley hired?" Aggie asked.

"No, the hired guard was the one you and I saw chanting with Claxley when we were hiding in the basement." Mallory turned to Kyle. "And he was also the person talking with Claxley outside the mummy room the night we hid there."

"Not Miss Snodgrass?" Kyle gasped.

"No, that was him you heard walking away in his heavy boots."

Aggie added more. "I also found out Eleanor Snodgrass has never been in cahoots with Claxley. Nor has she ever been after Emily Danner's position as curator. She apparently loves being a docent and interacting with the public. Wouldn't change it for the world, she said."

"Loves interacting with the public?" Mallory's eyebrows rose in disbelief. "You could have fooled me there."

Aggie laughed until Kyle asked Mallory puzzled, "So if Miss Snodgrass wasn't involved with Claxley, then what made her act all weird that day we went back to the museum to search for the ushabti?"

"Good point, Kyle," Ron interrupted. "I've been thinking about that myself and my feeling is that Claxley probably cast a spell on all the museum staff. One that would disorient them if anyone asked about the moving ushabti."

"I can believe that," Aggie nodded thoughtfully. She turned to address Mallory again. "So, what else happened with Nathifa last night, girl?"

"Well, here's the most amazing part of all," Mallory said, her eyes alight. "Just before everything disappeared I asked Nathifa who built the pyramids and the sphinx and she said there's not one sphinx, but *two*! Can you believe it? The second one is still buried in the sand. Said it's going to be discovered soon."

Ron fell back into his chair, his face a mixture of shock and excitement. "Seriously? Two sphinxes?"

"That's what she said."

"And the pyramids?" Kyle asked.

Mallory sighed. "The image dissolved before she could tell me more."

"Unbelievable," Aggie murmured.

"And one last thing," Mallory said placing the box Kevin had sent her on the table. She withdrew the armband and after everyone had finished admiring it, handed Aggie the note.

"This is your best mystery ever," Aggie beamed after reading the letter out loud. "Now I have a bit of news of my own."

She told them about Chief Banks's visit to the teashop earlier that afternoon. "I also learned that when Emily Danner came across Claxley doing his rituals in the basement that night, he was afraid she might report what he was doing, that's why he concocted the story about the missing museum pieces in the hopes she'd be fired."

"A master deceiver!" Kyle frowned.

"But here's the really good news," Aggie continued. "Because the Egyptian exhibit was such a success, Mr. Jarman is now making arrangements to bring in a Chinese exhibit from the Ming era. And he intends to have Miss Florentine make guest appearances to explain the history behind her family's collection of ancient Chinese pieces."

Mallory drew back in horror at the thought of all the strange ghosts an ancient Chinese exhibit was likely to bring with it. "Well if Miss Romano decides to take our class on a field trip there," she growled, "I'm calling in sick."

"Me too," Kyle said, slumping in despair. "Getting involved in the problems of ancient history is aging me."

The kitchen filled with laughter as Aggie stood to retrieve a tray of steaming hot cheese scones from the oven. "In spite of all that, we still make a great team," she called back. "A really great team."

From the corner of her eye Mallory saw the small stones in the armband suddenly pulsate in a shade of bright blue. Smothers also saw the glow and startled, reached with his paw to touch the piece of jewelry. His whiskers quivered and his fur stood on end as a surge of electrical energy ran through him. Thoroughly frightened he jumped from Mallory's lap and bolted from the kitchen, but distracted by the arrival of Aggie's hot scones, no one else appeared to have noticed a thing. Mallory quietly picked up the armband and smiled down at it knowingly. Perhaps Nathifa and her Prince might not be so far away after all.

ANCIENT EGYPT

Egypt was once lush with vegetation and looked nothing like the barren sand-covered land it is today. According to historians, the ancient Egyptian period lasted for more than 3,000 years between 2649BC to 332AD. It is divided into three main Kingdoms: the Old Kingdom, the Middle Kingdom, and the New Kingdom. During these periods, members of the same families (called dynasties) ruled as Pharaohs and Kings, often for hundreds of years at a time.

In the early periods of ancient Egypt only the Kings and Queens, along with their families, were given royal burials. Egyptians believed their pharaohs had a direct link to the gods and when they died, they would travel through the dangerous Underworld (a place they believe existed in an area directly below the earth) to reach the afterlife. Anubis (also known as the Jackal God) was the protector of funerals and tombs, and no public procession in Egypt was conducted without a statue or edifice of Anubis to march at its head.

To survive the dangerous journey through the Underworld, the royal body had to be preserved through mummification. He would also need many spells, passwords, and maps to help him on his journey to a new life. Egyptians tombs were filled with items to assist the tomb owner on the perilous passage to judgment, items that included such practical necessities as clothing, wigs, jewelry, hairdressing supplies, chariots, chairs, etc. The addition of sweet-smelling herbs and plants would help the jackal god Anubis sniff out the mummy and only let the pure move on to paradise.

Beginning sometime in the Middle Kingdom, copies of the Book of the Dead were placed in graves, along with ushabti statues. These ushabti figurines were believed to magically come to life and perform manual labor for the deceased. The Wedjat was a special amulet intended to protect the Pharaoh in the afterlife and ward off evil. Made in the shape of the eye of the falcon god Horus, one of ancient Egypt's oldest gods, it was either placed directly on the mummy or inside the sarcophagus (coffin).

Music in ancient Egypt played an important role in rituals, hymns and prayers. Professional musicians occupied a variety of social levels, the highest belonging to temple musicians, a position frequently held by women. These temple musicians enjoyed a close relationship with the royal household, as did other gifted singers and harp players.

Many types of instruments were used for praise singing, entertainment at court, and military events. The sistrum, a type of rattle that produced a clanging metallic sound, was especially important in religious worship. Many instruments including long flutes made of Nile bamboo have survived the ancient past, preserved by the shifting sands and extreme heat of Egypt's desert.

GLOSSARY

Afterlife

Where the ancient Egyptians believed they would live after death

Ammit

Ammit (also spelled Ammut) was the Devourer – the soul-eater who would condemn the deceased to oblivion if they could not pass judgment. Depicted as a mythological she-goddess with the head of a crocodile, the torso of a lioness and the hindquarters of a hippopotamus

Ankh

A symbol of immortality. It was the life-giver and used for protection

Antiquities

Ancient relics and artifacts

Anubis

The jackal-headed god associated with mummification

Arcane

Knowledge understood by few, mysterious or secret, a wizard who practices in areas that are dark, mystical, and obscure

Barge/barque

A canal boat that travels along rivers

Book of the Dead	An ancient Egyptian book containing spells and maps to help the soul find its way through the dangerous Underworld
Docent	A person who acts as a guide in a museum or gallery
Dynasty	Members and descendants of the same family
Egyptologist	Someone who studies the history of ancient Egypt
Halima	A female name meaning: *Gentle* (Egyptian origin)
Hieroglyphics	One of the written languages used in ancient Egypt
Horus	Ancient Egypt's best-known god, as well as its oldest. Usually depicted with the body of a man and the head of a falcon
Ini-Herit	A male name meaning: *He who brings back the distant one* (Egyptian origin)
Muse	A female musician who performed at rituals and sacred ceremonies
Nathifa	A female name meaning: *Pure* (Egyptian origin)
Pharaoh	A ruler in ancient Egypt
Portal	A doorway or entrance
Royal Tombs	Tombs for Pharaohs and Queens

Sarcophagus	A large coffin usually made out of stone, alabaster, or granite
Scarab	A dung beetle regarded as sacred in ancient Egypt
Sistrum	A U-shaped bronze framed musical instrument with a handle. When shaken the small rings on its movable crossbars produced a sound that ranged from soft tinkling to loud jangling
Sphinx	The huge stone statue found near the pyramids at Giza. It has a lion's body and a human or animal head
Underworld	A place filled with terrifying monsters and dangerous animals that had to be passed through before the deceased could reach paradise
Ushabti	Small statues buried with the dead and believed to magically come alive and help the deceased
Valley of the Kings	A valley in Egypt where tombs were constructed in the rocky terrain to bury the kings and powerful nobles of the New Kingdom
Wedjet	A symbol that represented the eye of the falcon god, Horus

Cedar Creek Mystery
Book One

Cedar Creek Mystery
Book Two

Available now from the following retailers:

ABOUT THE AUTHOR

Award-winning children's writer Anne Loader McGee has published numerous magazine articles for both children and adults. Her stories have also appeared in the *Los Angeles Times* and in online e-zines.

Anne's first novel in the Cedar Creek Mystery series, ***The Mystery at Marlatt Manor***, became a finalist in the 2009 Bloom Awards, and her Civil War story, ***Anni's Attic,*** won the Young People's Division of the International Peace Award. Anne is also co-author of the ***Sing Out Loud*** singing books for children.

Anne is a Master Graduate of the Institute of Children's Literature and a long-standing member of the Society of Children's Book Writers & Illustrators. She has studied writing at the American Film Institute in Los Angeles, and at the University of California and Los Angeles (UCLA). Anne is originally from New Zealand and now makes her home in Southern California.

VISIT HER ONLINE AT: WWW.ANNEMCGEE.COM

CPSIA information can be obtained
at www.ICGtesting.com
Printed in the USA
LVOW08s2301170217
524684LV00001B/4/P